The Adventure of the Scarlet Bird

By Ears O'Fluffin

Edited by Monica Yoknis

ISBN-13: 978-0-692-10945-8

Published by Two Oaks, LLC

Typesetting by Peacock Book Designs

This book is dedicated to Baggins the hamster, Boots the ferret, Andromeda the Great Dane, and many other beloved critters who wait on the other side of the Rainbow Bridge for us humans to join them.

CHAPTER ONE

The Pet Expo

◇◇◇◇◇◇◇

My hoomin had been planning this trip for months. It's only a three hour drive, and that's not so bad in my cozy basket on the seat, but I didn't like the idea of having to turn away clients or leave any cases unsolved.

"It's only four days, buddy, and there will be plenty of people and critters to watch," he folded his wiry frame into a squat to give me a reassuring pat.

"My mind craves stimulus, give me problems, give me work!" We animals understand hoomin speech, we just can't replicate it. Fortunately, the hoomin-pet bond allows my hoomin to hear what I telepathically send to him.

"Quote Sherlock Holmes all you like," he laughed. "This is an excellent opportunity to get my art in front of more people, and it's a highly targeted audience. I can't pass this up."

"Yeah, yeah, I know."

"Would you rather stay home with a sitter?" he asked, narrowing his steel gray eyes at me, quizzically.

My mind shuffled through memories back to the last time I had a sitter. Great Aunt Cora, all bright baggy clothes, and curly gray hair. She locked the pet door tight and forbade me from taking any cases. And she smelled funny. And she skimped on the treats. I shuddered at the disturbing flashback.

"Alright, let's go," I sighed.

"I thought so." He smiled as he stood, and started packing my travel kit. He's shorter than the average adult male hoomin, but being a "dwarf variety" myself, I didn't hold it against him.

The drive was alright, I slept most of the time. We spent Friday night in the hotel room, and my hoomin ordered a fresh salad for my dinner. Lettuce, carrot shreds, and cherry tomatoes. Not a bad addition to my hay.

My hoomin had an early breakfast, Saturday, so we would have plenty of time to go set up his booth. He spent some time debating if he should wear a tie. He'd styled his brown head fur more than usual, and traded his usual jeans for dark gray slack pants. He had brought what he called a "fancy shirt". Only thing I could see that was different about it was the more heavily starched cuffs and collar. Finally, he gave up on the debate with his reflection and came out to consult with me.

"What do you think, Ears? Tie? Or no tie?" He held the accessory in question up, then took it away.

"I'd say no tie," I didn't mention that I always thought the things looked ridiculous, anyway. "But maybe bring it, and put it on if you see others wearing theirs."

"Yeah, that makes sense. Thanks, buddy." He rolled up the tie and shoved it into a pocket of his "sport coat". I have no idea why hoomins call it that. I get that it's more casual than a "suit coat", but it had nothing to do with sports that I could see.

I hopped right into my carrier when he set it on the bed next to me. All of the items needed for the booth were still in the car, including my hat and coat. He set the carrier on the front passenger seat (my travel basket had become my bed in the hotel room) and drove around to the expo building's parking lot.

He carried me and my x-pen in first and set up the pen in a square next to his table. He set me and my carrier inside the pen and opened the door. I poked my head out.

"You can stay in your carrier, if you like, or look around the pen. Be best if you stayed in the pen, though."

"Right. I'll stay here."

He rushed off back to the parking lot to bring in more stuff. I stretched, allowed myself a yawn, and stepped out of my carrier. After a good ear scratch, a shake, and a bit of spot grooming, I periscoped up to take in the room. {Rabbits will stand on their back legs to get a better view, just like a periscope in a submarine.} It was enormous! The floor was covered in brown industrial low-pile carpet. Rows of tables were set back-to-back with cloth dividers. The dividers were more like curtains than walls. A heavy metal piping made up the frame, perhaps eight feet tall, and thick white cloth was stretched from top to bottom. There was enough cloth to create gathers on either end, leaving a wall that was pleasantly not flat, but looked soft and draped.

The sides of the fabric didn't overlap the sides of the frames, though, leaving gaps that a smallish critter could squeeze through. Each table was draped in a white cloth, and the name of each vendor was printed on a large sign on the back wall of the booth. I looked above our table, "Anderson's Art & Pet Portraits". Yup, that's my hoomin. Art is his passion, computer coding is his day job, and he's really good at both. Well, that's my opinion, anyway.

I turned toward the front door when I heard odd sounds approaching. He was coming back with a wheeled contraption full of boxes. Not sure where he got that, but it seemed more efficient than carrying the boxes. My office was on the top of the stack.

"Alright, buddy, where do you want to set your office?"

I looked at the back side of my pen and hopped to where I thought a good place was. About in the middle. He set it down on top of me, so I hopped out to see how it looked. Yup, that was a good spot.

The next item on the stack of boxes was my litter box. I hopped around to the back side of my office and pointed to the corner closest to the table. Just because I need it, doesn't mean it has to be out on display. I prefer to do my hay munching and pooping without an audience.

While I nudged my box and office into more precise positions, my hoomin opened the next box. This one held my desk and chair, the coat tree, and my hat and coat. He put the desk and chair in my office and suggested leaving the coat tree out where people could see it. I looked around and pointed to the front corner away from the table. He set the tree in place, then arranged my coat and hat on the pegs. We both looked at it for a moment. It just didn't seem right, there. Without a word, we both pointed to the corner next to the table. He chuckled and moved the tree across the pen. It looked much better there.

The last item in the box was a thing he calls a carabiner, a nearly egg-shaped hook with a spring closure. He clipped it to the side of the pen next to his chair. Out of his pocket, he pulled a gold chain that held the class ring that I'd dug up as a kit.

"I thought it'd be best to keep this close by me, so I can keep an eye on it."

"Sure, don't want anyone walking off with it." I would be a very unhappy bunny if that ring disappeared.

He clipped the gold chain into the carabiner and draped it carefully to rest against the inside of the pen. I could just reach it to boop it with my nose. {When a bunny pushes against someone or something with his nose, we call it a boop. This is a sign of affection from the bunny.}

I stretched out in the far front corner to watch my hoomin set up his displays. Once all of the boxes were emptied, stowed under the table, and the contents arranged, my hoomin scurried back out for the large display pieces. He came back with an official-looking hoomin, and they talked about how to hang the framed art on the divider wall. They reached an agreement and the official hoomin rushed off to get the hangers. My hoomin unwrapped the two large framed pieces. Official Hoomin returned with an armload of supplies, and they worked together to attach the hangers to the wall. Then, because four hands are better than two, they both carefully hung the heavy frames.

Both frames contained portraits. Of me. My hoomin says they're his best work. I can't argue, but I'd rather he not display the one of me as a baby. I guess I can see why hoomins think it's cute, but I'm not sure I like strangers seeing me all splayed out and wearing the ring like a bracelet. The other picture, now, that one I like. What they call a head-shot, three-quarters turn, with my coat and hat. Definitely the image I prefer to project. Tough guy, bun of mystery, serious and slightly brooding. None of this tail in the air, thumpers splayed out cutesy-ness. Oh well. If it draws in paying customers, who am I to complain?

As my hoomin walked away again, I saw him looking at his watch and muttering about having half an hour left. I shifted position so I could watch the other vendors and their animals set up their own booths. The aisles were arranged straight back from the front door and ran about half-way to the back of the room. At that point, the direction of the aisles changed to run crosswise. I'm not sure how many aisles there were, but by the rising din, I'd say a lot of people. It was fun to watch hoomins scrambling around, arranging and rearranging their tables and pets.

We were positioned two aisles left of the center of the front door, and roughly half-way back. The table to the right (as one faced our table) was inhabited by three Guinea pigs. Their hoomin was selling homemade piggy treats and hammocks. On the other side was a pair of love birds. Their hoomin was selling organic seeds and handmade toys. Across the aisle, I could see a pair of Yorkie dogs. The stuff on the table looked like fur-care products.

I looked back toward the door to see my hoomin bringing my water and pellet dishes. He set them down in front of where I was lounging. Without moving, I reached into my pellet dish to grab something to chew on.

"Feeling lazy, are we?" he smiled.

I just cocked an ear at him in response.

He stepped back to look at our booth. After a few minutes of study, he nodded and looked at his watch.

"Ten o'clock, buddy. The line out the door is already halfway around the block." He craned his neck to look at the doors. "Yup, they're letting people in, now." He looked down at me. "You ready?"

"Ready for the squeeing masses? {A squee is a human reaction to something cute, usually a high-pitched vocalization.} Oh, yeah. This is going to be great." I rolled my eyes.

"Well," he looked at me with that annoying parental head tilt, "if I sell a lot, I can upgrade your office again."

That got my gears turning. I wouldn't mind a wooden office. Cardboard is great, but it's just too tempting to bunstruct. {We bunnies like to take things apart. Hoomins have changed the word destruction into bunstruction to describe this natural tendency.} Wood would be more permanent.

It took a few minutes for people to make their way down our aisle. I remarked to my hoomin that I was surprised the kids weren't more intrusive with their hands. He reminded me that the local county fair was occupying the neighboring buildings. A lot of these kids were probably familiar with animals and knew how to be polite.

"Just wait, Ears, the city kids will be around this

afternoon."

I nursed a growing grump by chewing another pellet. I was about halfway to swallowing the pellet when I heard the first squee. It caught me by surprise, and my head involuntarily snapped in that direction. It was a short hoomin, blond with a chew toy stuck in its mouth. It started toddling over to me, its sticky hands reaching out for me. The adult I deduced was the mother tried reaching for it, but hoomin young are as slippery as their hands are sticky. I deftly hopped sideways out of reach, just as the hand pushed through the bars of the pen. The mother scooped the toddler up, gently telling her not to scare the bunny. She then turned to my hoomin, apologizing profusely. My hoomin was smiling at me. He'd just sat there and watched the whole thing. I drew myself up into the most dignified pose I could muster.

"That's OK, ma'am, no harm done," my hoomin assured her. The lady stayed a while, talking to my hoomin about his art. She bought a package of note cards.

When she left, I looked at my hoomin.

"Nice hop, buddy," he chuckled. "I love how you so cleverly turned a potential disaster into a sale."

"So glad I could help," I grumbled. He turned to talk to more hoomins, and I looked around for more dangers. Seeing none, I snatched another pellet from my bowl and settled in the middle of the pen. I've always been a fast learner.

The squees became intense when an adolescent female stopped in front of me and loudly proclaimed, "Oh em gee! That is the cutest thing ever, I mean, look at his little hat and coat!" This, of course, drew in more young females and more intense squees. I closed my eyes and flattened my ears, trying to ignore them. It didn't help. The noises drew younger kids, which drew their parents…. It wasn't long before I had a sizable crowd ogling me and flooding my hoomin with repetitive and inane questions.

"Is he really a detective?"

"Like, does he really solve crimes and stuff?"

"Does he really wear the coat?"

"What does he do when he can't solve a mystery?" I lifted my head to glare at that one.

My glare turned to smug satisfaction when my hoomin answered, "That hasn't come up. He's solved every case that's been brought to him."

"Aww, but he's too cute to be a detective!"

Ugh. I couldn't take it anymore. I stood up, turned my back, and flicked my feet at the crowd as I retreated into the privacy of my office.

I plopped my pouf into my antique "dollhouse" office chair and heaved a sigh. {A pouf, or poof, is a bunny's fluffy tail.} Trying not to resort to the bottle of carrot juice, I shook off my paws and rubbed my eyes. Figuring why stop there, I gave my ears a good grooming.

The sound of the crowd had died away, and I considered going back out there. I didn't just quote Holmes about needing stimulus, I really was bored. I needed a puzzle to work on. I sighed again, gave up, and pulled open my desk drawer.

CHAPTER TWO

The Client

◇◇◇◇◇◇◇

Inside the drawer were my two best friends, a pop gun that I keep loaded, and a bottle of carrot juice that keeps me loaded. I set the bottle on the desk and pulled out a shot glass. Carrot juice, for bunnies, is a lot like coffee for hoomins. Smooth and rich, it offers a sugar buzz, much like I've heard hoomins describe a caffeine buzz. It gave me a warm fuzzy feeling that made the crowds easier to tolerate. It didn't make up for a case to solve, though.

Maybe this Pet Expo idea wasn't so good, after all. My hoomin has had a lot of visitors to his table, already, and his art seemed to be selling well enough, but all I've gotten at my door has been squeeing hoomins. I've never had a biped for a client, and I'm not expecting one, now.

I had liked my hoomin's idea of bringing my office along. With my hat and coat hanging on the tree in the corner of my pen, and my shingle prominently displayed front and center above my door, I could hope potential clients would know I was open for business.

Now here I am, Ears O'Fluffin, Pet PI, slumped at my desk pouring myself a shot of carrot and it's not even 10:30 in the morning.

The orange liquid slid down my throat and hit my tummy with a warm tickle. I flattened my ears against my head in a pointless attempt to drown out the constant racket of the expo hall. There may not be a squeeing crowd outside my door, at the moment, but the room was not designed to dampen any ambient noise. This was going to be a long weekend.

A tapping on the roof of my office made me jump. Being a rabbit, jumping is one thing I do very well. So well, in fact, that I bumped my head on the ceiling. I count it a small miracle that I was able to keep the bottle from spilling.

Knowing that only my human taps on the roof like that, I poked my head out, and turned to glare at him. I wanted to make it clear that he would be seeing my fluffy cotton bottom the rest of the day. He smiled down at me, and said, "Ears, buddy, you have a visitor." I followed his gaze to the far side of my pen and stood stunned. Sitting just outside my pen was the most beautiful, most captivating, fluffiest cat I had ever seen. At first glance, she was pure white, her long flowing fur perfectly groomed. I expected her twitching tail to be white, but it had very faint tan stripes. I had never seen a cat like her, and I allowed curiosity to override boredom. I also noted that she was about three times my size. Not that that's saying much since I only weigh in at two and a half pounds. I may be small, but I am tough. Really.

Alert but relaxed feline eyes studied me from just

outside my pen. I pulled the rest of me out of my office and hopped over to my visitor. I noticed her eyes were a bright yellow-green, like the color of fresh carrot shoots. I swallowed a few times to get the taste of the carrot juice out of my mouf. {Mouth, kisser, trap, pie-hole, jaws, clam....}

I extended a paw through the pen, and she shook it gently.

"I'm sorry to disturb you, Detective O'Fluffin. My name is Tabitha."

"That's OK, Miss Tabitha, I was merely collecting my thoughts."

"And trying to escape the squeeing masses?" she smiled.

"That, too," I smiled back. "How can I help you, Miss Tabitha?"

"I need your help recovering something that was stolen from me."

"I'd be happy to recover your item. Why don't you give me all the details."

"Well, several years ago, another cat and I were rescued from a bad situation. I was adopted by a very kind and generous hoomin."

"And the cat you were rescued with?"

"He and I didn't get along very well, so the shelter adopted us into separate homes."

"I understand, please continue."

"My forever hoomin makes sure I have everything I need, but she is not wealthy. She sews and sells cat toys, but they don't make her much money." She pawed at the carpet, and her eyes left me to stare toward my food dish.

I could sympathize with her. "Unfortunately," I

sighed, "many hoomins prefer the cheapness and supposed convenience of mass-produced items. They don't seem to value the time, effort, and care that goes into handmade objects." This was a problem my hoomin lamented about often.

Tabitha looked back at me and smiled warmly. "Thank you. Anyway, my hoomin had saved up some money to get me something special for my Gotcha Day, this year. {The day a rescue critter is adopted. Not really a birthday, but can be celebrated as such.} A charm for my collar. That charm has now been stolen."

"What does it look like?"

"It's shaped like a flying bird and set with many small scarlet rubies. My hoomin says it sets off my eyes and looks very nice against my fur."

"That is a lovely gift. When did you last see it?"

"Last night, but you don't have to ask more questions."

"Oh?" I bristled a bit at her assertion. Asking questions is what I do. How am I supposed to solve a case if I don't ask questions?

"You see, I know exactly who took it, and where it is now."

I allowed my skepticism show.

She hurried on, "Really! His name is Shadow. He's here with his hoomin."

"And how do you know he took it?"

"He's the cat I was rescued with. We didn't get along because he's a bully. He would take all the food for himself, and not let me have any. He would attack me when I tried to use the litter box, and he would push me aside whenever a possible adopting hoomin came around. Now he is spoiled absolutely rotten. His

hoomin has lots of money and buys him everything.
He believes that only he deserves the best, and no one
else should have such nice things. Especially not me."
She paused for a moment. "Detective O'Fluffin, I'll pay
you a year's supply of any treat you name if you help
me get my scarlet bird back!"

That was quite an offer. I doubted she could really
pay it, but I was bored, and this offered something to
do. "Alright, Tabitha, I'll just get my coat and notepad.

"Sure, thank you!"

I hopped over to the tree and shrugged into my coat.
Then I went back into my office and stuffed my notepad and pencil into my pockets. Seeing the open bottle
of carrot juice, I replaced the stopper and set it back in
the drawer. My pop gun caught my eye, and I paused
considering if I should take it or not. This case seemed
strange enough, but I shook my head and closed the
drawer. Two steps toward the door, I stopped and
looked back at my desk. Finally, I let suspicion win,
opened the drawer and pulled out the pop gun. I heft-
ed it, feeling its weight, trying to convince myself that
I was just being paranoid. Finally, I shook my head,
checked that it was loaded, and dropped it into my
pocket as I headed for the door.

I booped great grandpa's ring and asked my hoomin
for an assist out of the pen. He picked me up, gave me
a quick hug, and told me good luck. I tooth-purred a
couple times as a thank you, and he set me on the floor.
{We bunnies have several signals for when we are happy. A tooth-
purr is when we quietly rub our teeth together. Same idea as a
cat's purr, different mechanism.} Tabitha met me in front of
my pen, and we set off toward the front door.

Along the way, I ran through my mind what I knew so far. This wasn't the sort of mystery I was used to solving. Normally, the thief was unknown, but here we had a clear suspect, and the client only wanted her jewel back. The only real mystery I could see was how to get the charm back without involving the hoomin law. That made me question why Tabitha's hoomin hadn't already called the police. Not wanting to go back to being bored, I kept my thoughts to myself. With nothing better to do, I might as well see where this was going.

We passed the central aisle and turned down the next one. The booth we ended up at was on the corner closest to the door. A highly visible and prominent location. Based on what my hoomin had told me while reserving his own booth, this one must have been quite costly to occupy.

"There," Tabitha nodded toward the table. "On the back table, curled up so smugly on his silk velvet pillow. That's Shadow."

Sure enough, an excessively fluffy black Persian cat was kitty-loafed on a rich dark green cushion. Maybe he was smug, maybe he wasn't, but he looked simply content to me.

"And there's my scarlet bird, Detective, right there in a display case. He's so convinced he deserves it, he had his hoomin put it in its own case," she snorted.

That seemed very bizarre, to me. This whole thing was getting stranger and stranger. A flood of questions flowed through my brain. Why come to me, and not the police? Why would someone steal something so unique at such a public event? And who, in their right mind, would prominently display a stolen item?

CHAPTER THREE

Baggins

◇◇◇◇◇◇◇

"Only a complete *cabbage* would display something he'd just nicked!" an emphatic voice with a distinct British accent announced behind me.

I spun around, looking for the owner of the voice. At first, I didn't see anyone. I'm used to having to look up for folks, it's very rare when I have to look down. I turned to face the voice's owner. He was a dark charcoal gray, almost black. Long hair was sticking out everywhere, forming a smoky aura around his trim little body. His arms were crossed over his chest, and his shiny black eyes were narrowed at Tabitha, openly suspicious.

I held out a paw, "I'm Ears O'Fluffin, Pet PI."

"Detective Baggins, British Pet Detection Service." He shook my paw firmly, and I could see that he was wearing a vest with bulging pockets.

I'd heard of the BPDS. Third-hand. In passing. Baggins was still eying Tabitha, but he also glanced meaningfully at me. Apparently, he had something to say to me and didn't want her to hear. Since I was becoming suspicious of the situation, myself, I wanted to know what he had to say.

"Tabitha," I turned to my client, "This is the point when I normally send my clients home while I investigate."

"But I can help you," she interrupted.

"Possibly, but given your history with Shadow, I think it best if you just let me handle the situation. Go back to your hoomin, and I'll take care of everything."

"Oh," she hesitated, "OK, I'll go. Good luck, and thank you for your help." She turned and stalked past the booth, glowering at Shadow. Once she was past, she trotted off toward the back of the expo hall.

As soon as Tabitha was around the far corner and out of sight, I turned to Baggins.

"I wouldn't trust that moggy, if I were you," he grumbled.

I could only assume "moggy" meant "cat", and smiled at him. "Oh, I don't trust her." He narrowed his eyes at me. "In my experience, critters who think you trust them are more likely to slip up and reveal more than they intend to." He raised one eyebrow. I continued, "I don't see any harm in letting her think she's got me snowed. For now, anyway."

Baggins let a sly smile cross his face. "Well, now. That's an interesting strategy. I'll have to remember that."

I gestured to the table across from the jeweler's booth. "Let's talk out of the traffic flow."

"Good idea." We both scurried across the aisle and ducked under the front of the tablecloth.

"You voiced my thoughts perfectly, Baggins, though

I admit I'd never considered cabbage as an insult."

He laughed, "Probably a British thing."

"Works for me," I chuckled. "So what brings you over here?"

"First thing, this morning, a green parrot knocked on our door. He said his name was Petey, and his hoomin's ring disappeared last night."

"Disappeared from where?"

"The table in their hotel room. His hoomin had left it there with other odds and ends, and gone into the water closet to wash her hands. Petey had occupied himself preening. When his hoomin came out to put the ring back on, it was no longer on the table."

I held up a paw for a pause. "Was the room door closed?"

"Excellent question! No, Petey's hoomin had propped it open with the slide bolt."

"Huh. What'd she do?"

"She blamed poor Petey. Was convinced he'd taken it. Apparently, Petey has a fondness for sparkly things."

"Many parrots do."

"I'd say most do, but he swears up and down he didn't do it. I asked if he had any idea who had, but he'd been preening, and saw nothing."

"Any scent trail?"

"Ah, great minds think alike, I see. Yes, there were two scents that lead from the door, up onto the chair, and onto the table. I followed them as far as I could, but they disappeared in the stairwell."

"Interesting. So what brought you to this booth?"

"I figured I'd check the booths selling jewelry, in case someone tried to sell it to one of them. I overheard your conversation with Tabitha, and had to say something."

"Sure, and honestly, I'm glad you did. Did you recognize the species the scent came from?"

"That's where it gets nutty. No, I didn't recognize it at all. Definitely not a dog or cat, or any other animal I've ever come across."

"So we have one real jewel theft, and one accused. Are they related? Has the ruby bird charm been stolen, and Shadow a cabbage? Or is Tabitha the thief and trying to use me as an alibi?" It was looking less and less like this would be a boring weekend.

"Or are there two thieves? The unknowns that took the ring, and Tabitha?"

"I know only one way to find out if someone is a cabbage...," I started.

"Talk to him?" Baggins finished.

"Yup. Let's go talk to Shadow."

We ducked out from under the tablecloth, and looked across to the green velvet pillow. Its feline occupant was gone.

"Where the thump did he go?!"

"Good question. Let's answer it under a table."

We scampered across and under the jeweler's table. Peeking out the back side, we saw Shadow at his water bowl. He looked up as we approached. I offered a paw and introduced myself, then Baggins.

"How can I help you, Detectives?" He seemed open and cheerful, but I make a point of not judging a book by its cover. Usually.

"We were noticing that lovely ruby bird in the case," Baggins gestured at the table top.

"Oh, yes, it is my favorite piece. My hoomin is so talented!"

"Could you tell us about it?" I asked.

"Of course, I'd be happy to!"

Before he could say another word, the room was plunged into darkness.

CHAPTER FOUR

The Theft of the Scarlet Bird

◇◇◇◇◇◇

In the darkness, a stunned silence filled the cavernous room. That didn't last long, of course. People
started shouting and a general din of confusion took
over. Shadow had pulled us under the back table with
him, so we would not be stepped on. Good thing, too,
as his hoomin rushed along the front table locking
cases.

"Well, Ears," Baggins asked, a mischievous glint in
his eye, "if you were a thief, when would you steal a
shiny red bird?"

"When the lights were out, and everyone was running around confused."

"Oh, you mean like…"

"Now!" we both snapped. I tried to lean out to see
the case in question, but Shadow's hoomin was still
rushing around, and I couldn't risk getting kicked.

Since I couldn't do much else, at that moment, I
spared a thought for my hoomin. I knew he'd be OK,
a dark room didn't concern him, but I hoped he wasn't
worried about me. Too bad the hoomin-pet bond

doesn't allow for long-distance communication.

The lights snapped on as suddenly as they had gone out. Less than a minute later, Shadow's hoomin shouted that the charm had been stolen, and called for the police.

I turned to Shadow and asked, "Can you think of anyone who would want to steal it?"

"I…no, I can't. I mean, why would they?" He looked genuinely shocked and confused.

"Where did it come from? Where did your hoomin get it?" Baggins asked.

"My hoomin designed and made it. He's made everything he has for sale here."

"So he's an actual jeweler, not just a seller?"

"Yes." Shadow sighed. "I should tell you all of it, since it will probably come out at some point."

"Anything you can tell us can be helpful," I assured him.

"My hoomin used to be a thief. Artwork, fancy jewelry, things like that. I'm not sure why, but something happened to make him want to change. He returned a lot of stuff that he'd taken and went to school to learn how to make jewelry. One day, he saw me at a shelter adoption event and thought I'd be a good companion. I could never have hoped for a better forever home. While in school, he started making things for me, as practice. The ruby bird was a final project for several of his classes. He graduated with honors and has had a steady business since."

"And no thoughts or temptations to get back in the game?" Baggins raised an eyebrow.

"No, of course not. I mean, why would he? If he

wants something, he can just make it…or something much better…himself."

"Sounds reasonable," I added, "that's about why my hoomin got into art. Can't afford a painting, make one you like better."

"I'm sure that's a common story, in this room," Baggins nodded. "I think we should examine the scene while scents are fresh."

"Agreed." I turned to Shadow, "If you can think of anything that might help, let us know."

"I will, and I'll let my hoomin know you are on the case. Good luck, Detectives."

We found a chair next to one end of the table, and I offered Baggins a ride up. He heaved a sigh and grabbed tightly to the back of my coat. I bunched up my thumper muscles and gaged the distance to the seat. Thankfully, I made it in one jump, and the next hop up to the top of the table was easy. Good thing gruff attitudes don't weigh much. The hoomin moved to stop us, but Shadow interceded. The hoomin nodded at us and turned back to the security guard he was talking to.

The display case was about 12 inches wide by 14 inches tall, and only three inches deep. The charm had been hanging on a small black nail, and the inside of the back of the case was lined with black velvet. Baggins sniffed around while I examined the case.

I started with the lock. It was a simple mechanism, very easy to pick with the right tools. The interesting clue was on the glass next to the lock…a paw print. I'd never seen a print like that, before. The fingers were long and thin, like a mouse or rat, but much larger than a rat. I studied the print, memorizing it. If we'd had more time, I would have sketched it into my notebook, but we needed to move as quickly as possible before the trail went cold.

"I caught a scent," Baggins announced from behind me.

"Great!" I left the jewel case to join him at the other end of the table. "What animal is it from?"

"No idea, but it's the same scent I found in Petey's room."

"Can't say I'm surprised." I sniffed where he indicated, so I could get the scent in my brain.

"Find anything on the case?"

"Just a paw print I've never seen before."

"Well, then, let's follow the trail and see what we're dealing with."

I crouched at the edge of the table, so Baggins could climb onto my back. Two quick hops and we were on the ground, sniffing for the scent trail. We followed it toward the front door, but paused at a chair against the wall beside the door.

"Ah," Baggins exclaimed, "here's the second scent from Petey's room."

I sniffed to pick up the second scent, but we couldn't figure out where it was going. I periscoped up to the seat of the chair. I followed the smell up onto the chair, up the back of the chair, and along the wall to a row of light switches.

"Well, now," I mused after rejoining Baggins on the floor, "it looks like we've got ourselves an acrobat for a suspect."

"Blimey!"

"Let's see where they went." We followed the pair

of scents through the crowd. Security guards were at
the doors, keeping people from coming in or going out.
The scent lead to the door on the far left. There was
no guard there, and the positive air pressure caused
by the building's air conditioning system held it open
just enough for us to squeeze through. Well, OK, for
me to squeeze through. Baggins had plenty of room
to spare. We paused when the full force of the summer sun hit our eyes. Were we really going to trail our
suspects outside into a busy fairground? A quick scan
around revealed a variety of dangers for small critters
like us. Tractors, hoomin crowds, dogs pulling against
their leashes…and those were just the things we could
see. The fairgrounds were on the edge of town, and
we could see open fields beyond the parking lots.
Cats, foxes, hawks…so many things out there to worry
about. I took a deep breath and glanced at Baggins.
He smiled, we nodded to each other, and put our noses
back to the ground.

CHAPTER FIVE

Going in Circles

◇◇◇◇◇◇◇

"Whatever these critters are, they can move fast," Baggins said between sniffs.

"And they're crazy agile."

"Don't think I'd like to face them alone."

"Me neither."

The trail lead us to a large pen with a packed dirt floor, where it disappeared under piles of smelly manure. I looked around the pen and counted seven sheep. I approached the closest sheep.

"Excuse me, ma'am?"

The ewe turned to me, hay dribbling from the corners of her mouth. "Yes."

"We were wondering if you had seen a pair of strange animals run through here."

"When?"

"Just a few moments ago."

"No, I've been eating, ask one of the others."

I looked at Baggins and smiled when he rolled his eyes. We moved on to the next nearest sheep.

"Excuse us, ma'am," I carefully approached the next

ewe.

"Aren't you supposed to be inside?" she asked.

"Yes, technically, but we are chasing two suspects in a jewel theft. We were wondering if you had seen a pair of strange animals run through here?"

"I saw them," a deep voice rumbled behind us.

We turned to see a large and burly ram.

"Capitol," Baggins rubbed his hands together. "What the devil did they look like?"

"Strangest critters I've ever seen," the ram looked around and lowered his head. "I've no idea what they were, but they looked like furry snakes."

"Furry snakes?" I was trying to picture that in my head.

"Yes, sir, furry snakes."

Baggins narrowed his eyes at the ram. "Snakes don't have fur."

"I know that, ya little fuzzball!"

It was all I could do to not laugh at the scowl on Baggins' face. If looks could kill…. "Could you possibly be more specific?" I asked the ram.

"Yeah, they were furry with long sinuous bodies. Short legs. Small round ears. Fluffy tails."

"Good, that helps a lot." I glanced at Baggins, he was still steaming. "Oh," I turned back to the ram, "did you happen to see which way they went?"

"Yeah," he swung his head toward the back of the expo building, "they went that way."

"Thank you very much for your help." I grabbed the back of Baggins' vest and gently pulled him away.

We recovered the scent trail outside the back of the pen, where it plunged into a forest of thick grass. In the distance, we could hear sirens approaching. Apparently, in this town, the police were not especially busy.

"I should have given that ram a pinch on his big nose," Baggins grumbled as we followed the scent.

"I don't think he would have noticed it."

"So? He still deserved it."

"Well, you are quite fuzzy. Probably the fuzziest critter I've ever seen."

"I know I'm fuzzy, but he didn't have to use it as an insult."

"True, he didn't."

"Especially when we were questioning him about a suspect," Baggins snapped.

"Good point." I was failing to keep the amusement out of my voice.

"And like you should talk, cotton ball butt!" The vibrant green grass was so tall and thick he basically disappeared into it.

I laughed. "I don't think I've ever heard that one, before."

"Ha!" He finally gave up scrambling through the jungle and crawled up onto my back.

I was able to move much faster but was still grateful when the trail came out of the grass onto a concrete sidewalk.

The trail lead around to the back of the expo building. About a quarter of the way along the back wall, both scents disappeared under a solid door. We looked up, trying to decide how to open the door, only to discover that it did not have a knob on the outside.

"What the bloody heck good is a door without a handle?!" Baggins squeaked.

I was beginning to think that hamsters have two settings, annoyed and furious. "It's for security proposes," I sighed.

"Hang security! How did our suspects get in?"

"I'd bet they had someone waiting on the other side for them. Probably their hoomin." I sniffed around for a hoomin scent.

"Fantastic." Sarcasm was clearly one of Baggins' finer talents. "What are we supposed to do now?"

"Well, we have two options," I plopped my poof down to rest.

"I'm all ears."

"We can run back to the front door, through the hall, and find this door on the inside."

"Or...."

"Or we wait here until someone opens the door."

Before Baggins could come up with a sarcastic response, the door opened. A hoomin came out, a cigarette in his mouth and a lighter in his hand.

"Like that," I chuckled as we dashed through the door.

As the door closed behind us, Baggins looked at me. "You're good."

"What can I say, I got four lucky rabbit's feet." We both had a good laugh at that, then returned to sniffing out the scent trail.

CHAPTER SIX

Dead End

◇◇◇◇◇◇◇

The trail ran right along the line of cloth-draped tables parallel to the back wall. Roughly halfway down the aisle, the scents made a sharp left into the open floor. They disappeared completely in the middle of the aisle. That made no sense, where could they have gone?

"Spiral search?" Baggins asked.

"Yup."

We started on opposite sides of the spot the scent disappeared. Moving counterclockwise, and staying directly opposite each other, we put our noses to the ground and sniffed carefully as we spiraled outward. We stopped when we got to the tables on either side of the aisle. I looked across to Baggins. He just shrugged.

I hopped across to meet him. "How do two animals simply disappear?"

"They can't," Baggins shook his head.

"Right, so where did they go?" I scratched my right ear.

"They must have gotten into a carrier, and their

hoomin carried them away," Baggins gestured toward the far corners of the vast space.

I nodded. "Reasonable."

"I wonder…" he muttered, gazing at my ears.

"Hmm?"

"If I stand on your head, and you periscope up…"

"Okay, go on." I was pretty sure I knew where he was going with this.

"I might be able to catch their scent in the air."

I looked at him skeptically.

"That'd at least give us a direction to go."

I considered that for a moment. I couldn't find much of an objection, but I doubted he'd find anything. Since I couldn't come up with a better idea, I lowered my head to let him climb on.

"OK, now stretch up as far as you can," he urged.

"Right, hang on."

He grabbed the tips of my ears, and I periscoped up onto my tiptoes. I could hear him sniffing the air, and feel him turning in a circle on top of my head. I almost fell over when he shouted.

"There! That way. Let me down."

I lowered my chin to the floor and he jumped off. He started off in the direction we had been going. There was a gap in the row of booths, providing a shortcut into the next aisle. Baggins paused to sniff the air again, then turned and ran through the shortcut.

I hopped along, keeping up easily. "I don't smell them."

"Not them, specifically, but one like them."

"Oh, I see your thinking, find out what they are, if nothing else."

"And maybe this new one knows where to find others."

"Perfect."

Baggins lost the scent as we came out the other side of the shortcut.

"Blast! I can't tell which direction to go, now," he snarled.

"Let's split up, then."

"Good idea. Can you whistle?" he asked.

"Yeah, you?"

"Yup. First one to catch it, whistle."

"Got it," I nodded. "I'll go left."

I turned left and made my way to the middle of the aisle. There were a lot of hoomin feet to dodge. Problem was, they were so busy looking at the goods in the booths that they weren't paying attention to where their feet were. I gave up sniffing while zigzagging, so I spent the time reminding my brain of the sort of scent I was after. I stopped in the middle of the aisle to periscope and sniff. Since the hoomins tended more toward the outsides of the aisle, I had a relatively empty slot to stand in. Turning a full 360 degrees, I only caught a very faint scent. It was definitely coming from the direction Baggins had taken. I turned all the way around again just to be sure.

A faint whistle drew my attention back toward the shortcut gap. I looked around, realizing that finding a hamster in a sea of hoomins is much like finding a needle in a haystack. The former was certainly far more pleasant than the latter, despite his innate grumpiness. A second whistle caught my left ear and allowed me to home in on his location. I started hopping in that direction, figuring we'd find each other as I got closer.

When I got about three booths down on the other side of the gap, I caught sight of him crouched under the corner of the next table. I allowed myself a chuckle as it occurred to me that, without the vest, he'd look like an overgrown dust bunny. I choked off the chuckle as I got within earshot, figuring he wouldn't appreciate the comparison.

"You find it?" I asked as I came up beside him.

"Definitely. Two booths down, opposite side. Still the third scent. I'm pretty sure there's only one, but I didn't want to approach it myself."

"Sounds good. Let's go see what we're dealing with."

We stayed right up against the bottoms of the tablecloths, keeping the screen of hoomin legs between us and the mystery critter. We stopped across the aisle from our quarry. Not knowing the nature of these animals, our instinctive tendencies as prey species overrode our investigative boldness. As we watched, the critter came out of a cozy hidey house. I understood what the ram meant by furry snake. That's essentially what the new critter looked like. Long and slinky, lots of fur, and short legs.

"What the thump is that?" I asked.

"I have no bloody clue."

"Guess there's only one way to find out."

"I can think of another way," he sounded a bit more nervous than I felt.

"Ask our hoomins?"

"Yeah. Mine has her tablet with her."

"Mine, too. I'm not sure I want to leave this lead, though."

He made a noise that was part scream, part growl,

part sigh, then said, "Fine, let's go talk to it."

As we got closer, I could see more detail in the animal's coloring. It was actually quite lovely and reminded me of the opossum I'd met. The fur was a very pale cream, almost white, but the tips of the long guard hairs was a silvery gray. The whole effect was a shimmering pale lavender. Very nice.

The owner of this shimmery coat noticed us approaching, and sat quietly to wait. The closer to the pen we got, the closer Baggins got to my side. I half expected him to try to hide under my trench coat, but he never got quite that close. I didn't mind, and I certainly didn't think any less of him for it. That nervous instinct is what keeps us alive, after all.

I went ahead and took the lead as we stopped a few inches from the wall of the pen.

"Excuse us, could we have a few moments of your time?"

"Of course." The voice was distinctly female, as well as warm and gentle. "Are you investigating the theft?"

My head jerked back and my ears pitched forward. I did not expect that from this critter. I'm not sure why, as I think back, surely the news of the theft had circulated around the whole building by now, but I was still caught off guard.

"Yes, ma'am, we are."

"Do you have any suspects?" She seemed genuinely curious and excited about the situation.

A small punch in my side told me that Baggins found this suspicious, and I couldn't argue.

"We do, in fact. Two individuals with scents and descriptions very similar to yours."

"Oh dear. Well, I can assure you I would never steal anything…well…except maybe my hoomin's slippers," she giggled.

"I'm glad you limit your stealing to hoomin footwear, ma'am…"

"My name is Layla."

"OK, Miss Layla," I continued, "we were hoping you could help us out with something."

"Sure, I'm happy to help," she skipped around a bit with excitement.

"Neither of us has ever met a critter like you…"

"What the bloody heck are you?" Baggins blurted from my side.

I rolled my eyes and Layla laughed. I'm glad she wasn't offended.

"I'm a ferret," she smiled. "A member of the weasel family."

"A ferret, interesting. I've heard of your kind, but you're the first I've ever met," I smiled.

"We're not the most popular pet animal. We can be quite mischievous, and tend to get into things," she lowered her eyes bashfully.

"I see. Do you know if there are other ferrets around?" I asked.

"I've seen a few, but I have no idea how many are here."

"Any idea where we might find some of the others?"

"No, I'm afraid not. The few I saw were in their carriers as their hoomins were coming in, this morning. I didn't see where their final destinations were."

"Alright. Well, thank you, ma'am, for your time and help."

"Certainly, I'm glad I was able to answer at least a

few of your questions."

We took our leave of the lovely Layla, and headed back for the shortcut gap. I stopped in a safe spot at one of the corner tables.

"Well, isn't that just dandy?" Baggins asked.

I was beginning to think that hamsters had elevated sarcasm to the level of a fine art. "Well," I offered, "at least we know what they are."

"I'd gladly trade 'what' for 'where'."

"Yeah, me too," I took a deep breath and puffed it out.

CHAPTER SEVEN

The Needle in the Haystack

◇◇◇◇◇◇

I looked toward the front door and realized that we were looking down the same aisle that Shadow's booth occupied. There were several uniformed police standing around the booth and one that looked to be a detective.

"Probably questioning the hoomins that were standing around when the lights went out," Baggins observed.

"That's where I'd start."

"Me too."

Looking around the gigantic room, I couldn't help lamenting that our haystack just got a lot bigger.

"On the drive out here, my hoomin mentioned that there were over two hundred vendors just at this pet expo. That didn't include the rest of the fair."

"Yeah, it was big enough for my hoomin to justify the trip from England," Baggins nodded.

"Now I don't feel so bad about the three-hour drive we took."

"I slept most of the flight across the ocean. Nothing

much to see, anyway."

"I can't imagine being stuck in a carrier that long," I closed my eyes tight at the thought.

"That's why I slept."

I nodded in sympathy.

"I think I remember my hoomin saying she counted ten different species, just at this expo," Baggins marveled.

"I can believe that."

"That's one heck of a haystack." He sighed and plopped on his butt.

I looked down at him, and couldn't help grinning.

"What are you smiling at?"

I couldn't keep it in, anymore. "You look like an overgrown dust bunny," I laughed.

"Oh yeah?! Well, you look like an oversized cotton ball with sloppy eyeliner!" He tried to keep an offended scowl, but finally gave up and we shared a friendly laugh.

We had needed that tension release. The best way, I've found, to get over feeling overwhelmed is to laugh about it. Convince your brain that the situation is absurd, have a good laugh about it, then take another look at it from a different perspective.

Baggins and I both rubbed our faces and shook off the lingering frustration.

"Alright, Detective O'Fluffin, where do we go from here?"

Taking a deep breath, I thought back to my training. I let out the breath in a puff.

"We ask questions," I turned to my partner.

"Alright, then," Baggins nodded. "What do we

know, so far?"

"We know that there are two suspects."

"And that they worked together," he held up one tiny finger, "one dousing the lights," up came a second finger, "the other nicking the gems."

"We know that they are ferrets," I added.

"And we know they are in the building."

"Do we know that for certain?" I closed my eyes tight at the question.

He thought for a moment. "Fair enough. I do think we can reasonably assume that they are in the building unless the security guards are complete cabbages."

"Very true." I couldn't help the image of a cabbage-headed hoomin in guard uniform popping into my head. "Anything else we know?"

"Not that I can think of," he shook his head.

"OK, then, what else can we assume?"

"That they are here with a hoomin."

"Yes. And that their hoomin is a vendor." I looked around at the near-by hoomins.

"Why can we assume that?"

"Have you seen any visitors with their animals?"

He looked around. "Now that you mention it, no. I hadn't really paid that much attention. I've been busy looking for our suspects."

"Me too, but I noticed it, this morning."

"Alright, their hoomin is a vendor, since a visitor with a pet carrier would draw attention."

"Right. Also, I think we can assume that, whatever her motives may be, Tabitha is not involved with these two ferrets."

He gave me a side-eye glare. "What makes you think that?"

"I'm pretty sure I would have noticed an unfamiliar scent on her when we first met. Also, I have not picked up her scent anywhere as we've been following the two ferrets. I'm not saying it as a certainty, but I think it's a reasonable assumption."

Baggins sat thinking about that. I could almost see his teensy little gears turning. Finally, he nodded, "OK, it's a fair assumption."

"At least for now."

We sat thinking, but I couldn't come up with any other assumptions. The question now was, how does one find a needle in a pile of hay? Other than eating all the hay, of course.

"What we need now is one of those guidebooks," Baggins had, apparently, been thinking along the same lines I had.

"Guidebook?" I grinned.

"Yeah, one of those smallish books people have been carrying around. I looked at it with my hoomin, last night. It's mostly vendor and sponsor advertisements, but there's also a map that shows the layout of the room. The numbers on the booths correspond to the numbers in the vendor list. That's how my hoomin knew how to find our booth."

I thought about that and did remember my hoomin looking at one, while he was eating breakfast. He didn't say anything about it, so I didn't think much of it. Then I thought of a potential problem. "How does the vendor list help? The shop names people use rarely mention their pets."

"True. Thankfully, the people who made up the guide book were kind enough to include the species that would be at the booth with their hoomins."

"That is helpful. So where do we find one?"

"If we don't happen to see one on the ground, I'm sure we can pilfer…I mean borrow…one," he smirked.

We split up and looked around on the ground, hoping to find one handy. I stopped in my tracks when I heard a sound reach my ears. It was the peculiar sound that magazines make when they hit the floor. I looked around and saw a guidebook laying in the middle of the aisle. I'm certain it hadn't been there thirty seconds before.

"Thank you, clumsy hoomin," I whispered as I made my way through the hoomin feet to the book.

I caught Baggins' attention and pointed him to the other side of the aisle. He nodded and started making his way over to me.

"Where'd you find it?" Baggins asked.

"Someone dropped it right in front of me."

"Huh. Got a guardian angel, do you?"

"Something like that," I chuckled.

We flipped to the middle of the book, where the map was located. Baggins looked at it a moment, then turned it to line up with the direction of the doors. I pulled out my pencil and we started scanning the list for ferrets. As we were looking, a thought occurred to me. Like Baggins, many of the vendors were from a lot further away than my three-hour car ride. The show was only for Saturday and Sunday.

"Everyone will be leaving on Monday," I sighed.

"Worse than that," Baggins added, "my hoomin said that some leave Sunday afternoon."

"Oh, pewps!" {Poop, crap, dung, feces, fertilizer, meadow

muffin, night soil....}

"Of course, the police might make them stay. I'd assume that, if they haven't caught the thief, they'd make everyone stay until they do."

"That makes sense, but will also mean a lot of unhappy hoomins."

"Especially for those of us with transatlantic flights to catch."

"Right. No pressure, or anything."

"Absolutely none."

As Baggins read off ferret-occupied booth numbers, I circled them with my pencil. In the end, we had nine booths circled. We were able to cross off Layla's, leaving us with eight. At least, now, we had target areas in our haystack. Of course, that didn't solve the problem that the haystack might start blowing away in 24 hours, taking the needle with it. We did have some help from the hoomin police, knowing that they would keep people around until they had at least a real solid lead.

"I wonder how far the hoomins have got?" I mused.

"Not far, I'd say, they were still at Shadow's booth, when I looked down that way."

"Good, with any luck, we'll have an answer before they waste anyone's time with a search."

Before Baggins could comment, the public address system squawked to life.

CHAPTER EIGHT

Police Search

◈◈◈◈◈◈

"ATTENTION, LADIES AND GENTLEMEN! THIS
IS DETECTIVE CAMPBELL OF THE BOROUGH-
VILLE POLICE DEPARTMENT. AS YOU MAY HAVE
ALREADY HEARD, THERE HAS BEEN A THEFT
IN THE BUILDING. A VERY VALUABLE PIECE OF
JEWELRY HAS BEEN STOLEN FROM ONE OF THE
VENDORS. WE WILL BE CONDUCTING A BOOTH
TO BOOTH SEARCH FOR THE STOLEN ITEM,
SHORTLY. VENDORS MUST RETURN TO YOUR
BOOTHS, WITH YOUR ANIMALS, IMMEDIATELY.
ALL MEMBERS OF THE VISITING PUBLIC, PLEASE
CONCLUDE YOUR CURRENT TRANSACTIONS
AND PROCEED, CALMLY AND ORDERLY, TO THE
FRONT EXIT. YOU WILL BE SEARCHED AND IF
NOTHING IS FOUND, RELEASED. THERE WILL
BE NO RE-ENTRY TO THIS BUILDING AS WE CON-
TINUE OUR INVESTIGATION. AGAIN, VENDORS
AND YOUR ANIMALS RETURN TO YOUR BOOTHS
IMMEDIATELY. CUSTOMERS, CONCLUDE YOUR
CURRENT PURCHASES AND MAKE YOUR WAY TO

THE FRONT ENTRANCE. THANK YOU FOR YOUR COOPERATION."

"Bugger!" Baggins spat.

"Agreed. OK, we only really need this one page, right?"

"Yeah, as far as I can tell."

I used my nails to pry open the staples holding the guidebook together. The map page came out easily, and I folded it to fit in my pocket. Well, I tried to get it in my pocket. I ended up holding it in my mouf.

"OK, Baggins, I'll give you a ride to your hoomin, then head back to mine. Hop on," I lowered myself so he could climb up onto my back. He grumbled the whole time.

"Alright, cotton ball, I'm ready."

"Good, hang on." I grabbed the folded page in my mouf, and took off running.

"Watch it!" Baggins shouted as I dodged a hoomin.

He tried to offer other "back-seat-driver" instructions. I pretty much ignored him, and focused on hopping, running, leaping, zigging, and zagging as fast as I could. Baggins' booth was at the far end of this first crosswise aisle. The going became more difficult as the hoomins were becoming anxious about being searched. They tend to pay even less attention to their feet the more nervous they get.

I felt Baggins start to slide off a few times, but he had a firm grip on my coat and managed to recover his seat. The shouted instructions dissolved into frantic hammy screams as a large stroller blocked my path. I didn't see a way around it, so I flopped onto my belly and dove under the carriage, between the wheels. We slid out the other side, and I got my feet back under me without breaking stride. Baggins' terrified screams morphed into cheers and shouts of encouragement.

I could see Baggins' booth ahead, only three more to go. His hoomin was standing behind the table, looking for him. She looked worried. That worry turned to relief when she caught sight of us dashing through the crowd. Just then, a hoomin toddler dropped to the floor, right in front of me, in full-blown tantrum mode.

"Jump, rabbit, jump!" I heard Baggins shout.

I planted my thumpers on the carpet, dug in with my nails, and launched us into the air. Baggins let out an excited whoop as we sailed over the kicking and screaming child. I was glad that he had the sense to shift his weight, minuscule as it was, as far back as possible. Because of that, I landed a lot softer than I had feared, and was able to easily make the last few strides to his waiting hoomin. She had dropped to her knees and scooped him up for a kiss. I dropped the paper so I could catch my breath.

Baggins hopped down and grabbed the paper. "I'll keep this, so you can get to your hoomin."

I nodded. "Thanks. What floor is your hotel room on?"

"Third."

"Mine, too. Let's meet at the ice machine, after dinner."

"Good idea, see you then."

I took a deep breath and nodded a "see you later" to Baggins. He nodded back, and I turned to backtrack to the shortcut aisle. Since hoomins were now filling the middle of the aisles, I stuck to the outsides. I slowed as I turned the double right around the end of the row.

The left turn down our aisle was a little more difficult, as I had to cross the stream of hoomins. I paused on the far side since my hoomin's booth was on the right, and I only wanted to cross the river of feet once. It was a few seconds before I spotted a gap caused by a hoomin on his phone. I growled at the twinge in my back foot as I pushed off to sprint through the line.

Why must hoomin police always make things harder than they needed to be? Why must they always interfere in an investigation? We were so close to a solution in this case, and now we have to drop everything so they could plod through their grossly inefficient official procedures. That was the true source of the animosity between the officials and us private investigators. We weren't bogged down by the red tape of formal procedure, so we were able to get our answers faster. They envied us this freedom and often seemed to delight in dismissing our work.

I saw my hoomin standing in front of my pen, looking for me. When he saw me running down the aisle, he knelt to meet me. I hopped right into his waiting arms and settled into a relieved snuggle. He carried me around, sat on his chair, and set me on the table.

"Let's take your coat off, buddy."

I stood and let him pull the coat from my shoulders, then resumed my exhausted loaf while he rehung it on the tree. I settled into a rhythmic, meditative nose twitch, willing my heart to slow. My hoomin helped by stroking my head and ears.

"I'm glad you didn't get stepped on when the lights went out," he whispered.

"No," I told him, "I was already under a table."

"Good. You know anything about this robbery?"

He stopped petting me so I could stretch and yawn. I like to think I look intimidating, like a roaring lion, when I yawn. Sadly, it usually induces chuckles and a squee from hoomins. I shook off my paws and rubbed my face to come out of the partial trance, then told him the whole thing from the beginning. I made sure to give him every minute detail since he would have to relay that information to the police. Life would be so much simpler if I could tell them, myself, but the hoomin-pet bond doesn't work that way. An animal can only "speak" to his or her own hoomin. All pet parents know about this special bond. Unfortunately, hoomins who don't have pets have difficulty accepting what the pet parent tells them. There was a very real chance that the police would simply dismiss what Baggins and I had learned because they doubted the truth of the bond. Oh well, no harm in passing on the information, what they chose to do with it made no difference to me.

"Baggins had said to leave the map with him so I could get here faster, but now that I think about it, it was a genius idea. It gives him something physical to show them to corroborate what I tell them."

"That is pretty clever. I'm glad you're not working alone, on this one, buddy. It's a huge place and a seriously bold thief. Better to have a partner watching your back." He pulled a handful of hay from a bag and set it on the table in front of me.

I grabbed a mouthful of hay and chewed enthusiastically. We were both startled when a hoomin stopped in front of the table.

"Excuse me, is this bunny Ears O'Fluffin?" the stranger asked.

"Yes, he is."

"Awesome. A lady over there asked me to find you and give you this note."

"Lady?"

"Yeah, Sue. Over at Ocean's Bun & Hammy Emporium."

"That would be Baggins' hoomin," I told my hoomin.

"Yes, of course," my hoomin took the note. "Thank you!"

"Sure thing." The stranger melted back into the stream of hoomins shuffling toward the door.

My hoomin opened the folded note. "She says Baggins needs to know what you're going to tell the police detective. Wants me to text her."

"We didn't have time to discuss that, unfortunately. Let them know that I plan to tell them everything we did and learned. I see no point in withholding anything."

"Makes sense to me." My hoomin spent some time composing the text, then sent it off.

A few minutes later, we got a response, "Baggins agrees, and thought it'd be good for him to show them the map to corroborate what Ears tells them."

"Great idea. Good luck," my hoomin responded.

We watched as the police searched each booth. There were two detectives leading two teams of uniformed officers. One of the teams had a police dog with them. The presence of the dog gave me some hope that they would be more accepting of what Baggins and I had to tell them. I had mixed feelings about that. This had the potential to be the biggest case of my

career, and here were the cops butting in. They generally don't like to share the credit for solving mysteries,
so part of me wanted to tell them nothing. On the
other paw, hiding information from official hoomin authorities was generally not a good idea. I really didn't
want to cause any troubles for my hoomin, or Baggins'
hoomin, for that matter. As much as the contrarian
side of my nature wanted to refuse to do their work
for them, I had to stand by my plan to tell them everything. I could not let my hoomin get in trouble for the
sake of my ego.

The search was painful to watch. I know they were
trying to be thorough, but they were really glaringly
inefficient. Someone needed to teach these hoomins
how to search. Better yet, how to induce a guilty being
into giving itself away. I reminded myself, with a
heavy sigh, that they go to Police Academy, not Private
Investigator's Academy. A lone investigator has to
work much differently than one who has the bureau-
cratic machinery of the local PD behind them. We have
to be far more flexible, and can't rely on intimidation
to get what we want. As I watched, I could tell the
police detectives were relying heavily on their ability
to threaten legal punishment on the hoomins they were
questioning. I even overheard him ask, "Is it really
worth going to jail for?" Ugh, sloppy.

I watched more closely while they examined the
booth next to ours. I was disappointed that the team
with the dog had gone the other way. It would have
been much better to talk to him. Oh well.

Finally, the detective approached our table. He held
out his hand to my hoomin.

"Detective Campbell, Boroughville PD."

My hoomin stood and shook the detective's hand, "Scott Anderson. This is my buddy, Ears O'Fluffin, Pet PI."

"Ah, yes. I've heard of Mr O'Fluffin," his voice oozed contempt.

I flattened my ears, he didn't even glance at me. My hoomin gave me a quick pat to remind me to behave myself and not take it personally. Ha! Of course I'm going to take it personally. However, I have carefully cultivated the ability to remain professional in such situations. I sighed and let my ears pop back up.

Detective Campbell continued, "Where were you at 10:43, this morning?"

"I was right here, ringing up a sale."

My ears perked up, and I looked around to see what was no longer on the table. There was one less of the 11 by 14 prints in the rack. I was so happy for my hoomin, that I gave my tail a little shake.

"Really, you can be that specific?" Campbell asked skeptically.

"I certainly can, Detective. I was swiping the card," he held up his phone with the little white square attached, "when the lights went out. A few minutes ago, I pulled up the record of the sale, and it listed as going through at 10:44 am."

"Uh huh. Could I see that record, please?"

"Of course." My hoomin tapped through the screens to the transaction in question and handed his phone to Campbell.

Campbell jotted down the name and address of the customer in his notebook. Reasonable, but tacky.

"And where was your rabbit at that time?" He still didn't look at me.

"Ears was questioning Shadow, the cat to whom the stolen charm belongs. They were under the table the jewel case was sitting on when the lights went out."

Detective Campbell stared at my hoomin for a few seconds. "And why was he there?"

"A white cat had come by, asking for his help recovering a stolen charm. He went with her to see the animal she was accusing of stealing it." My hoomin continued to explain everything that I had told him, including about Baggins.

"Wait, a hamster?!" Campbell was incredulous.

"Yes, a hamster. Apparently, he's pretty well known over in England."

"How is a hamster supposed to investigate any-thing?" Campbell sneered.

"Same way a bunny does. Same way a police dog does. They ask questions, interview witnesses, and look for clues." I was proud of my hoomin for keep-ing his calm, and not backing down. I gave his hand a nosebonk.

"Right. I don't suppose the rabbit and the hamster know who these ferrets are?"

"Not exactly. They had marked all the booths with ferrets on the expo map, and were about to start inter-viewing them when you're announcement sent them back to us."

"Right."

"Baggins kept the map. He's with his human, over in the second cross-wise row," he pointed in the gener-al direction of Baggins' booth.

"Uh huh. Well, I'll be sure to talk to him about that," Campbell rolled his eyes.

This whole time, I had been watching the uniformed

officers search our booth. Thankfully, they were careful with the framed art and the larger matted prints, but they made a royal mess of my stuff. Spilled my pellets everywhere, sifted through my litter box, spread my hay everywhere (that's my job, thank you very much), and completely upended my office. They even searched my coat pockets and desk drawers.

"Has your rabbit come up for an explanation for WHY ferrets would steal a piece of jewelry?"

My hoomin sat, so he wouldn't be looking so far down at me. "Well, buddy, how about it?"

"I'd bet carrots their hoomin put them up to it. I've no doubt ferrets have a special love for shiny things, I mean, who doesn't, but most critters would go for easy to get stuff. Only a hoomin would go out of anyone's way to steal from a locked case in a crowded room."

"Makes sense, to me." My hoomin stood and relayed my answer to Detective Campbell.

"Right," his voice dripped with a sick mixture of sarcasm and contempt. "I have to agree that we're looking for a human offender. Given that, I see no reason to consider two ferrets to be of any real help to this investigation."

My hoomin shrugged, putting his hand on the top of my head. "How you conduct your investigation is up to you, of course. All Ears can do is share what he and Baggins have learned. What you do with the information is your choice."

"Yes, it is."

"Excuse me, Detective," one of the uniformed officers butted in, "we didn't find anything."

"Good. Alright, Mr Anderson, thank you for your cooperation. We're telling everyone that all vendors and their animals are to remain in town until we inform you otherwise."

"Sure, I understand that."

"And tell your rabbit he and his rodent partner better not interfere with this investigation. Understood?"

"Of course, I'll let them know to stay out of your way."

Detective Campbell and his officers moved on to the next booth. He never did look at me.

I sat glaring at Campbell. My hoomin sat down and started petting my head and ears. Finally, I sighed and settled into a resting loaf.

I must have fallen asleep because the PA system startled me.

"ATTENTION, LADIES AND GENTLEMEN, THIS IS DETECTIVE CAMPBELL. WE HAVE COMPLETED OUR SEARCH. WE MUST INSIST THAT YOU ALL STAY IN TOWN UNTIL WE INFORM YOU OTHER-WISE. YOU WILL BE RELEASED TO RETURN TO YOUR LOCAL LODGINGS, SHORTLY. WE WILL ALLOW THE PUBLIC TO ENTER DURING POSTED SHOW HOURS, TOMORROW. HOWEVER, EVERY-ONE WILL BE SEARCHED AS THEY LEAVE, TO ENSURE THE STOLEN ITEM IS NOT PASSED ON TO A CONFEDERATE. WE ASK THAT, AS YOU LEAVE, TODAY, YOU TAKE WITH YOU ONLY ESSENTIAL ITEMS. WE WILL SEARCH YOU AND YOUR ANI-MALS AT THE DOOR." There was a pause, presumably as Campbell conferred with his officers. "YOU MAY BEGIN MAKING YOUR WAY TO THE FRONT DOOR, NOW. THANK YOU."

"Glad I thought to bring you two sets of bowls and two litter boxes, huh, buddy."

"Definitely."

"What are you going to need for tonight?"

"Just my coat. Baggins is going to take me to see his client's room. We'll see what we can find from there."

My hoomin set my carrier on his chair and grabbed my coat. He checked to be sure my notebook and pencil were in the pockets, then draped the coat over my carrier. He pulled the white square from his phone and set it on the table behind a stand of art prints. The phone, he put in his pocket, and he set his tablet computer on top of my carrier.

"Ready, buddy?"

"Ready."

He picked me up, kissed the top of my head, and put me in my carrier. When he was sure I was all the way in, he closed the door, picked up the carrier, and started toward the front door.

Being searched a second time was annoying, but thankfully brief. We walked across a weedy field to the hotel's side door. My hoomin used his key card to unlock the door. He trudged up the three flights of stairs, and down the hall to our room.

"I'll prop the door open, so you can leave when you're ready." He opened the carrier, o let me out. "Do be careful about not getting in the way of the local police, please. I really don't want you and Baggins getting into trouble."

"Don't worry. I doubt we'll get very far, anyway. I just want to see his client's room. It's unlikely that we'll find all that much useful."

"Good. How about a nice dinner salad?"

"Yes, please!"

CHAPTER NINE

In the Hotel

◇◇◇◇◇◇◇

Dinner arrived quickly. My hoomin got an egg salad sandwich, and I got a salad with spring greens, carrot shreds, cherry tomatoes, and cucumber slices. No dressing or onions. Everything was crisp and fresh, and I munched happily.

After dinner, I sat on my hoomin's lap while he surfed the TV channels. After the third time around, he turned the TV off with a heavy sigh and tossed the remote to the other side of the bed. I stretched, crawled up his chest, and gave him a quick kiss on the nose. {Bunnies kiss the same way dogs do, we're just more civilized and less sloppy about it.} He smiled, gave me a hug, and set me down on the floor. I pulled my coat on and checked my pockets.

"Good luck to you both," he said.

"Thanks. I don't know when I will be back. If we do catch a trail, we'll follow it."

"Sure. Do try to be back before morning, though, huh?"

"Right. Like I said, I doubt we'll get very far."

"OK, be careful, buddy."

"Of course," I smiled and squeezed out the partially open door.

The ice machine was next to the elevator, about half-way down the hallway. Hotel hallways are horrible places to try to find a specific scent. Especially around room service distributed meal time. So many scents were overlapping, that I wasn't sure I'd be able to follow my own scent back to the room.

I found Baggins curled into a little hammy loaf under a corner of the ice machine. "I hope you haven't been waiting long, Baggins."

"Baggins? Who is this Baggins you speak of? I am merely a dust bunny. We dust bunnies have no names. We are the nameless, faceless horrors that gather under furniture, waiting for the day when we will unite to overthrow the ruthless hoomins."

I wasn't sure how to take this odd little tirade, so I just stood there gaping at him. Finally, he raised one eyebrow, and I broke up laughing. He chuckled with me for a few seconds, then resumed his normal serious and gruff demeanor.

"Well, I'd say the local constabulary waisted what could have been a perfectly good afternoon."

"Definitely. The detective didn't even acknowledge my presence."

"He didn't mine, either."

"So it's up to us, but we'd better darn well stay out of his way."

"HA! As effectively as they are 'investigating', I don't see how we could possibly get IN their way."

"Probably not, but we should at least not let them see us if we can avoid it."

"Agreed. So, what now?"

"I'd like to see your client's room if we could."

"Sure, he's down on the second floor."

We looked up at the elevator call button. Then we looked at each other. We both shook our heads and started off toward the stairs.

Petey had an impressive travel setup. Three perches made of different things, set up at three different heights and joined by either rope or ladders. Hanging off one perch was a soft hiding house, that was really more like a covered hammock. He had an array of colorful toys dangling or sticking up, most of which had bells or other noise-making abilities.

When we got into his room, he was resting on his hoomin's shoulder as she typed on her laptop computer. He fluttered down to the floor to meet us, as we entered. I have limited experience with birds as pets, so I'd never met an Eclectus parrot, before. He was mostly a bright emerald green but had a line of electric blue along the leading edges of his wings. Under his wings was a rich, velvety red. To contrast these primary colors (when speaking of light, red, green, and blue are the primary colors; whereas when speaking of pigment, magenta, cyan, and yellow are the primary colors...I would explain further, but my editor insists we avoid such bunny trails) his beak was a garish mix of orange and yellow.

"It's good to see you again, Detective Baggins. And you must be Detective O'Fluffin?" he greeted us warmly.

"That's me," I smiled.

"I told Ears about your problem, and he wanted to

have a look at the scene," Baggins explained.

"Of course, of course. Don't mind my hoomin, she's telecommuting. She's not really ignoring you, she's just focused on what she's doing."

I looked at Petey's hoomin. She had a wire leading from the computer to her ears. A contraption my hoomin calls 'earbuds'. It generally meant that the hoomin has turned off her sense of hearing. Must be nice to be so far up the food chain that one can simply ignore a fifth of the information coming in from one's surroundings. Oh well, it allowed us the safety of talking to Petey in his room.

"Baggins told me about the theft," I said, turning back to Petey. "But I'd appreciate it if you would walk me through what happened."

"Certainly." Petey walked toward his perches, and Baggins and I followed. "I was on the middle perch, there. My hoomin had finished setting up my stuff, and let me out of my carrier onto the bed. She offered her hand and pulled me close for a quick snuggle, then held me out so I could hop to a perch. I stretched and shook off, then started preening. I always give myself a really good preening after a ride in the carrier."

I smiled. "Me too, to be honest."

"Who doesn't?" Baggins asked.

"My hoomin had picked up the phone to call room service," Petey continued, "and started pulling her stuff out of her pockets. After she hung up the phone, she stuck her wallet and stuff in her computer bag, and took her jewelry off…"

"One moment," I interjected, "where was the computer bag?"

"On the chair she is sitting in, now. The jewelry, she

set on the table."

"Whereabouts on the table?"

"Next to the bag, near the edge furthest from the door."

"Good, thank you," I nodded.

"Sure. She went into the hoomin potty room, and I heard her running water in the sink."

"And the room door was open?"

"Well, kinda. It was exactly like it is, now. Propped open with that lever thing."

I was, of course, familiar with this practice, as my own hoomin does it. It seemed a bit odd for a hoomin female traveling alone. "Any idea why she left it like that?"

"Oh. Hmm. Not really. I'd guess because she knew the room service guys were coming. I can ask, later, after she's done with her work."

"No, don't bother her over it, I was just curious," I shook my head and smiled.

"OK. Anyway, she was running water, and I started working under my wings. It took me a while because it was a long car ride. I heard the water stop, and when I looked up, she was coming out with the towel. She looked at the table and stopped. She kinda just froze there. It seemed odd, so I looked up again from what I was doing. I looked where she was looking and saw that the table was bare."

"Completely bare? Like, everything was gone?" This surprised me. A smart thief would only take one item, expecting it to take longer before it was missed.

"Yes, totally bare. She muttered something I'm not allowed to repeat and rushed over there to look. Then she bent down to look on the floor. When she stood up, she had her necklace and earrings, but not the ring. She turned to me and asked what I'd done with her ring. I insisted I hadn't left my perch the whole time, that I was busy preening. She gave me that look, I'm sure you know the one, that said she didn't really believe me."

"Why would she suspect you?"

"Well. I can't deny that I really like sparkly things, and I'd played with her ring, before," Petey looked down at the floor.

"I see. Please continue."

"I insisted that it wasn't me and that I hadn't been anywhere near the table. She finally believed me but wasn't sure what to do. She asked if I'd seen or heard anyone. I said I hadn't, since the water was on and I had my head under my wing. I am sure it wasn't a hoomin, though. I would definitely have noticed a hoomin coming in."

"Most likely, especially since he would have had to push the door open."

"Exactly. It must have been a small critter, who could have come through the door without opening it. I remembered my hoomin saying that Detective Baggins would be at the show, this weekend and that his booth would be close to ours. I suggested that I talk to him in the morning. She agreed and closed the door," Petey shrugged.

"I see the second chair, there. Has that been moved?"

"No, it was just like that."

"Thank you. I'll have a look around, if that's OK?"

"Sure. Just please don't disturb her."

"I'll be as unobtrusive as I can."

"Thanks."

I hopped back to the door to start sniffing. Baggins followed but stayed back so I could work. The carpet was hopeless for scents. Too much time had passed. The chair, on the other hand, was more helpful. It took me a few minutes to sort out all the smells, but I did catch a whiff of the same two scents we had been following all day. I was able to catch some on the table top, as well. They had definitely crawled up onto the chair and jumped up onto the table. The fact that they were able to do that without drawing Petey's attention was impressive. Sure, he had his head under his wing, but birds see movement very well, and I was surprised that he hadn't caught the movement out of the corner of his eye. Not that I thought any less of him. None of us can be one hundred percent alert all the time.

"Well?" Baggins came up behind me.

"The floor is hopeless, it got vacuumed today. The chair and table both still have their scents. Definitely what we followed today."

"I can accept that they weren't heard, but some-one had to have seen them, at some point. Two furry snakes slinking along a hotel hallway can't be a normal occurrence."

"I can't argue with that. I wonder if the hotel has cameras in the halls?"

"Maybe, but they certainly won't show it to us."

"No. We'll have to leave that to Detective Campbell. Assuming he even thinks to look."

Baggins turned back to his feathered client. "Did your hoomin tell the police about the ring?"

"Yes, when they were searching our booth."

Baggins nodded as he turned back to me. "Well, I

suppose we'll just have to let the local constabulary figure out security footage."

"Unless, of course, we solve this whole thing first," I grumbled.

"You don't like him, either, I take it?" he laughed.

"Not particularly."

"Alright, what next?"

"I'm wondering just how good of a job the maids do at vacuuming the hallway."

"Oh?"

"If I was going to run down a hall and sneak into a room, I'd stick as close to the wall as possible..."

"...And if the housekeepers don't vacuum right up against the wall..."

"...There might still be some scent left for us to follow."

"Capital idea, let's go have a sniff."

We thanked Petey for his time, and bid him good night. Out in the hall, we split up and sniffed along the wall on opposite sides of the door. I had gone towards the elevator, and Baggins went towards the stairs. I smelled nothing like our suspects and was about to cross to the other side of the hall when Baggins called back to me.

"Here, I've got them!"

"Really?" I made my way over to where he was resting a teeny white hand on the wall. There was a strip of carpet on the wall, about four inches wide. Obviously, the hoomins had put it there to protect the wall against the rubbing of the vacuum cleaner, but it was also perfect for holding a scent if one rubbed up against it. I sniffed the strip where Baggins pointed

and found the scent right away. There was no doubt
that these were our suspects.

Baggins was continuing down the hall, sniffing along
the strip of carpet. After a few feet, he broke out into
a trot. I gave up my own sniffing and hopped to catch
up. He stopped when he got to the door leading to the
stairs. We sniffed around in expanding circles, trying
to relocate the trail. I started up the stairs, sniffing
along the left side. After not finding anything by the
third step, I crossed to the right side and worked my
way back down.

"They didn't go up," I announced.

"Nope, they went down. I've got them, here." He
was on the second step down, on the right side. "You
know, Ears, I think this trail is fresher than twenty-four
hours."

"I was thinking the same thing. More like only a few
hours."

"Or less."

"Yes, or less."

"Shall we follow it down?"

"Yeah, I'm curious, now."

"You mean you weren't before?" he had a mischievous gleam in his eye.

"OK, OK, now I'm MORE curious."

We worked our way, one stair at a time, down to the
ground floor. Here, the scent trail crossed the landing
and disappeared under the outside door. I looked
out the glass pane door, into the orange-lit back parking lot. Beyond the parked cars, I could see a strip of
landscaping. Some short-mowed grass, a few trees,
and a small flower bed. Just at the edge of the pool of
light left by the street lamps, I could just make out the

tall grass and weeds of the field my hoomin and I had crossed earlier.

"Well, now what?" Baggins asked impatiently.

"Wait till morning, I suppose."

"Really? You're gonna come this far, and not keep going?"

"You really want to go out there? In the dark? There's wild fields all around this area. There are sure to be foxes, maybe coyotes, and certainly owls."

Baggins looked out the door. He took a deep breath, puffed up his chest, and asked, "So?"

"What, you want to be someone's dinner?"

"Anyone thinks they want me for dinner is gonna have a fight on his paws! I'm no one's dinner, rabbit, and neither are you. We have a job to do, and a fresh trail to follow."

"Where could they possibly be going, out there? They aren't wild ferrets. They won't just disappear into the vastness of the prairie. They must come back at some point, tonight."

"True, but suppose we find them, tonight? Suppose this trail leads us to their secret stash of stolen sparklers? How many more thefts might we solve, and possibly before Campbell and his bobbies even know about them?"

It was my turn to pull in a deep breath. As I let it out, slowly, I could hear my great grandpa's voice, *"Remember, Ears, there's no reward without risk."*

I puffed out the last of the deep breath. "OK, let's do it!"

"Fantastic! Now, how do we open the door?"

"I have an idea about that. I think I can jump up and grab the lever. If I do it hard enough, the lever should go down and the door open."

Baggins eyeballed the door, then me, then broke up laughing. He curled himself into a little laughing ball of fuzz. I stopped glaring at him long enough to see a hoomin coming toward the door. I grabbed Baggins by his vest and pulled him into the corner. The hoomin was talking on his phone and didn't even notice us. He pushed the door wide open and hurried through it. Throwing caution to the wind, I pulled Baggins out as the door was swinging shut.

CHAPTER TEN

Carnival

◇◇◇◇◇◇

We waited in the recess of the doorway and watched as the door closed softly. The problem of getting back in didn't occur to me until I heard the lock click closed. The thought bounced up, unbidden, that our luck had to run out eventually. I shook it away and looked at my partner. He sat, staring wide-eyed into the darkness.

"Still sure this is such a good idea?" I asked.

"Yes," he squeaked. He cleared his throat and tried again, "Yes, I'm sure."

"OK, then. You sniff around, and I'll keep lookout. I'm taller, so I'll see things first."

"I like that idea." He sniffed around the recess to find the trail. "Here. They stayed close to the wall out here, too."

"Sensible. Lead on."

Baggins started off along the wall, toward the far end of the building. I followed a few steps behind, keeping eyes, ears, and nose peeled for even the slightest hint of danger. It took a while before I got used to the idea of my reflection in the bumpers of the parked cars. Every space between and under the cars could have been hiding a predator. I reached into my pocket and gripped the handle of my pop gun, thinking as I did so that it might not help against a large and hungry wild carnivore.

I was so focused on our surroundings, that I bumped into Baggins when he stopped. Thinking he had spotted something I hadn't, I whispered, "What? What's wrong?"

"The trail leaves the wall, at this spot." He sniffed around, the trail leading him closer to the cars. "Yes, they went out into the car park."

"Figures. OK, let's go. I'll keep watch."

"Good." Baggins followed the trail, slower, now.

I considered whether it would be better for me to go ahead of him, but dismissed that pretty quickly. He'd be a sitting duck behind me. With me following, I could keep an eye on him, and any predator would see that I was looking out for him.

We stopped again at the back ends of the cars. I looked carefully for anything that might be lurking. When I was reasonably sure there wasn't anything, I looked down at Baggins. "Where to, now?"

"Across, as far as I can tell. I'd rather not dawdle across."

"Agreed."

"How about I hold your coat tail. You can keep watch while I sniff, and I'll tug your coat the direction we need to go. That way we'll be close together out in the open."

I thought that for a second. "Sure, that makes sense." I took a step out from the shelter of the cars and felt Baggins take hold of my coat.

We walked together fairly quickly. The trail seemed to be going straight across, as was sensible, and Baggins didn't have to steer me much. We paused for a breath next to the nearest tire. After a few moments of rest, we nodded at each other and Baggins sniffed around for the trial. I followed as he lead along the cars, toward that strip of landscaping I'd seen from the door.

The trail went up the curb and into the flower bed. Our suspects must have taken a break to play around in the flowers because the two scents split up.

"Bugger," Baggins muttered. "Just stand here, I'll see if I can find them together, again."

"Right." I periscoped as tall as I could, so I could see over the flowers, and listened as Baggins scurried around among them.

Finally, he called from a few feet behind me, "Here it is. They started across the grass here."

I worked my way through the flowers to the edge of the lawn, then skirted the bed to where Baggins waited. "More open space, huh?"

"Yeah. They probably headed across the field, back toward the fairgrounds."

"What the thump for?!" We could hear a constant, droning, noise coming across the field. It was the sort of noise logical animals avoided. I periscoped up, but couldn't see anything beyond the sea of tall grass and the apparent slight rise of the field.

"I can think of three possible reasons," Baggins mused.

"Three? I can come up with one…they're nuts!"

"Yes, that's one. The other two are, they're going to

meet a fence to get rid of the loot before the police find it, or they are going to stash it somewhere for the same reason."

I took a deep breath to consider Baggins' other two ideas. I let the breath out in a puff. "OK, I can see that. But neither of those rule out the first."

Baggins chuckled, "I can't argue with that."

"Question now is, are we nuts enough to keep following them?"

"I want to find them. I want to recover the jewels before the local bobbies." He paused. "I'm not nuts, Ears, and I don't have a death wish. But I also don't want to go back to my hoomin and have to tell her…or my client…that I was too scared to follow the thieves as far as I possibly could." He paused again. "Do you?"

I screwed my mouf around a bit, then sighed. "No, I don't. Alright, let's keep going."

We crossed the green lawn quickly enough but paused again at the edge of the weedy field. Here the grass and weeds were much taller, and I could barely see over the tops. Thankfully, the trail was easier to follow. It was no longer just a scent trail, but the grass had stayed parted where the two ferrets had gone through. We now had a more physical trail to follow.

The grass behind the sheep pen this afternoon had been long, but this was worse. I had to devote more focus to navigating the jungle than I would have liked. Poor Baggins was scrambling through a jungle of tall grass and thorny weeds. He maintained a long string of uniquely British epithets aimed at the offending vegetation. We made very slow progress until we came to a hub of crossing trails. There we had to stop altogether.

"Oh, brilliant!" Baggins shouted. He sighed and scrambled around sniffing for the scent.

The ground in the middle of the hub was bare dirt. The grass around this bare spot was trampled quite flat for about two feet on every side. I counted six different trails of varying sizes, not including the one we had been following. Finally, Baggins beckoned me to the far side of the hub.

"They went this way. Still making their own trail, as far as I can see."

"Alright, let's keep on, then."

Baggins huffed a sigh and pushed on. "My kingdom for a machete."

"I don't think they make hamster sized machetes, Baggins."

"Why not? I've got a hamster-sized magnifying glass!"

"Yeah, and how many times would you have to hack at one of these grass blades before you got through it?"

He stopped to examine one of the offending stems. "I don't know, two or three."

"More like three or four. Then how would you get around the falling stem?"

He stopped and turned to glare at me. "You and your logic can just go take a hike!" That apparently wasn't enough, so he stuck his tiny little tongue out at me.

When I laughed, he hissed at me, then went back to scrambling through the jungle of grass.

The droning noises were getting louder as we worked our way across the field. The closer we got, the more distinct sounds I could make out. There were several different strains of music. Well, what could possibly be called music. It was like the tune the ice cream truck plays. But louder. And much more annoying.

It wasn't long before the noise was too loud for me to possibly hear anything sneaking up on us through the grass. I had to shout so Baggins could hear me. "Can you hear anything, at all?"

"Like what, the things we would want to hear before it pounced on us?" he shouted back.

"Yeah!"

"No, I can't. You?"

"Not a thumping thing."

I resigned myself to relying on sight and smell, but even smell started to go away. The air was becoming filled with a bizarre mixture of popcorn, hydraulic oil, and something so sweet I could feel my teeth rotting in my head. I tried to convince myself that no wild predator would bother to come anywhere near this sensory overload. Unfortunately, foxes, owls, and other wild hunters weren't the only dangers out here. Loose dogs, cats, and hoomin children were just as hazardous, and far more likely to be around in this racket.

I heard Baggins mutter something, but couldn't make it out. "What?" I asked.

"I said, blimey!" he was standing on the edge of the field, holding the last two blades of grass apart.

I stepped right up behind him and looked over his head at the most horrific sight I've ever seen.

Bright lights of every color imaginable were blinking, flashing, whirling, and spinning. Hoomins were wandering around everywhere, and children were squealing and running back and forth. Many other bizarre and disturbing smells wafted over us.

"What is all this?" I asked.

"I remember my hoomin mentioning a carnival at the fair. Apparently, for whatever reason, they only do this at night."

"For bun's sake, why? How can they stand the lights and the noise?"

"Apparently, some hoomins actually enjoy such chaos."

"Hoomins, yes, I can see that. But why would our suspects come here?"

"They're more likely to get trampled than find a fence. And I doubt they could find a decent hiding spot that wouldn't be found by the workers when they clean up."

"I can't argue with that. Maybe they're here to do more thieving?"

I thought for a minute. "Yeah, that's possible. So what do you think we should do now?"

"I'd still like to follow their trail as far as we can. Maybe we'll get lucky."

"Right. Or maybe we'll get squished."

"How did that work across the car park, with me holding your coat?"

"I thought it worked OK, you?"

"I thought so. Should we try it again?"

"Sure."

Baggins grabbed my coattail, and we set off across the hard-packed dirt toward the nearest vendor tent. The ferrets had taken the same route, but we had to stop and regain the trail when we got to the back of the tent. This vendor was selling flavored kettle popped popcorn, and the smells of caramel, cheese, and cinnamon were overwhelming.

The scent trail took us to the right, away from the field we'd come out of. I made sure to catalog landmarks in my mental map, so we could find our way back again. I doubted we could trust our own scent trail, so I made sure to have a backup up map in my head.

Three tents down, the ferrets' trail turned to run between tents, and toward the flow of hoomin foot traffic. We followed cautiously, trying hard to not be seen. I stopped at the front corner of the tent, staring at the constant flow of hoomin feet. The swirling and blinking lights were dizzying here. The chaotic mix of sounds flooded over us like a wave, and I could feel a knot growing in the pit of my stomach. This was not a good place for a dwarf bunny and a horrible place for a hamster. I felt Baggins shudder beside me, and he edged closer to my side.

"If that doesn't give you a case of the collywobbles, I don't know what will."

"The what?"

"Collywobbles. Jitters. Heebie-jeebies."

"Right. Of course, collywobbles." I guess you really do learn something every day.

"What say we head back to our hoomins and report our findings?"

I had to smile at his effort to maintain a brave, cool exterior while essentially saying he wanted to run home to his mommy.

"Definitely. They will be wanting an update." The idea of a long snuggle and a good night's sleep was a good one, but I wasn't about to admit I wanted my daddy if Baggins wasn't. I may have mentioned that I'm a tough guy.

Together, we retraced our steps along the backs of the tents and back to the trail through the tall grass. We paused at the edge of the field, so I could scan for dangers. I was somehow able, over the racket behind me, to hear a sound that chilled me to the bone. I'd only heard it in the wild once, on a camping trip with my hoomin. After we'd gotten home from that trip, he played recordings of other calls from the same animal, so I could recognize them again. I picked up Baggins and dove into the tall grass, away from the trampled trail.

"What are you…" he protested. I clamped a paw on his muzzle to silence him.

"Shh," I whispered, "listen."

I stood up just enough to poke my ears above the grass, and willed my heart to stop pounding. Ironically, I hoped to hear it again. If they were calling, they weren't actively hunting. If there was more than one, they were having a discussion over territory, and we had a better chance of getting across alive.

Baggins had his back against my belly, standing on his tiptoes, straining to hear what had alarmed me. I turned my right ear to the far right side of the field. There it was! That distinctive *hoo-h'HOO-hoo-hoo*. Very faint. I wished I could convince myself that he was far enough away to not be a threat, but with all the other noise filling the night, I had to reject it as fantasy. Keeping my right ear locked in that direction, I scanned with my left ear, waiting to hear a response call.

Kraawk. There! Across the field, toward the hotel. Again, call…*hoo-h'HOO-hoo-hoo…*, and response… *Kraawk.* Thankfully, I only heard two. From what my hoomin had read to me, this was likely a mated pair calling to each other. What I was less sure of was, if they're calling, are they hunting? I'd guess not since everyone knew where they both were. Best to chance it, and not wait until they were quiet.

I turned to face the hotel, and the direction we needed to go. Listening more, I could pin the male to our three o'clock, and the female to our ten o'clock. I squatted so Baggins could hear me.

"Owls?" he asked.

"Yeah, Great Horns. Big."

"Hunting?"

"I doubt it. As long as they're talking, I don't think they'd be hunting."

"Makes sense. How far away?"

"With all this other noise, I can't tell. The female is closer, but not in the direction we need to go. I think we should make a run for it, but stop and listen again at the crossroads."

"Good idea. Could I bum a ride?"

"I was just going to suggest that." I lowered myself to the ground, so he could climb onto my back.

He settled down, testing our collective balance. "OK, I think I'm ready."

I took a deep breath and forced it out. "Here we go."

With one hop, I pushed through the grass and back onto the trail. I planted my front paws in the middle of the trail and twisted to put my thumpers down on the far side. As soon as I felt solid ground, I pushed off again, sending us down the trail. I kept trying to

force myself to think this was just another Bunny 500
in the yard. The only real difference, I tried to convince
myself, was that binkies were not allowed in this race.
The more practical side of my brain, however, insisted
on bringing up the fact that the female owl's call was
getting louder, as we got closer to the hotel. I was only
able to fight panic because her relative position didn't
change.

I wasn't able to hear the male's call, while I was running, so my imagination insisted on constructing the
scene of him dropping down on top of us. The reali-
zation that Baggins would suffer the full force of that
attack made me feel bad that he was the most exposed
of the two of us. The fact that there wasn't a better way
to travel as fast as we needed to was small consolation.

"I see the crossroad, just ahead," Baggins announced
from my back.

I slowed as I approached the opening, then dove into
the tall grass just beside it. Baggins slid off my back,
while I caught my breath. He stood up on his toes,
facing the direction the female owl should be. *Kraawk.*
We both heard her. Definitely closer, but now at our
nine o'clock. I didn't think she had moved. Standing
slowly, I poked my ears above the grass to listen for the
male. A much fainter *hoo-h'HOO-hoo-hoo,* reached my
ears. Apparently, he hadn't moved, either.

The question now was, which trail is the right one?
I had thought, as we had come through earlier, that
I had drawn my mental map well enough to get us
back easily. Unfortunately, sitting there in the dark,
I realized that the map had been useless. All the trail
entrances looked alike. Several lead back in the general
direction of the hotel, but we knew that at least one of

them would lead far closer to the female owl than we wanted to go.

"We'll have to sniff it out," Baggins whispered.

"Apparently so," I sighed.

We stuck close together, crouched as close to the ground as we could, and slunk across the opening. Moving left to right, we sniffed the entrances of each trail, trying to find our own scents. We hit jackpot at the fourth trail. I periscoped up to listen. I heard both owls, apparently still in the same places.

"OK, hop on," I laid down and waited while Baggins crawled up.

"Ready!"

I launched us down the trail and watched as the pool of light from the street lamp grew closer. I slowed to a stop before we got to the edge of the field. We would have to use the cars for cover, and I'd have to sprint across the open lot.

Baggins slid off, again, and was listening. "Ears," he whispered, "I don't hear her, anymore."

"What?" I popped my ears up, again.

Kraawk. We both flattened ourselves against the ground.

"By Peter's ghost," I whispered, "she's in the tree right above us!"

CHAPTER ELEVEN

Day Two

◇◇◇◇◇◇◇

Flattened to the ground and huddled against each other, Baggins and I considered our next move. One of the advantages of being a rabbit is that you can see above you without turning your head. I scanned the tree branches, but couldn't make out where the owl was. I heard the male in the distance, but his mate didn't return the call. I knew, in the pit of my stomach, that she had gone into hunting mode.

A flutter drew my attention to one of the middle branches. Yes, there she was, I could just make out her silhouette against the street lamp. Her great yellow eyes seemed to glow in the darkness.

"Do you see her?" Baggins whispered.

"Yes. She staring straight at us," I whispered back.

"Did she see us?"

"Most likely."

"So. We're doomed, then?"

"I don't…." I stopped when I heard a large animal running towards us from the left. It sounded like a large dog. I squeezed my eyes shut, expecting to feel coyote fangs dig into my back. I started when the sound of running was replaced by barking.

Opening my eyes cautiously, I saw that the dog had front paws on the tree trunk, and was barking up at the owl. She ignored the dog, for a while, but the barking didn't stop. I heard a hoomin calling from the far end of the parking lot, "Dromie! Dromie, shush." The dog stopped barking and came sniffing over to us. Baggins pressed even closer to my side.

"What are you two small ones doing out here?" The concern in the dog's voice was comforting.

"We were investigating a crime," Baggins grumbled.

"Oh, are you the detectives working the theft from this morning?"

"Yes, ma'am, that's us," I tried to keep my voice steady. It wasn't easy. We had a four pound, sharp-taloned bomb waiting to drop on us. Now we had a hundred pound, fanged canine asking us questions.

She must have sensed our concern (alright, I'll admit it) terror, because she lay down next to us, shielding us from the owl's direct line of sight. If the owl wanted to swoop down on us, she would have had to get past the jaws of a Great Dane to get to us.

"It seems you gentlemen are in a bit of a predicament. Would you like an escort back to the door?"

I spoke up before Baggins could say something snarky, "Yes, ma'am, we would be very grateful for an escort."

Our new friend's hoomin walked up to us, cautiously. "What's the problem, Dromie? Who have you got there?"

In response, she looked up into the tree. It didn't

take the hoomin long to spot the owl. He waved his
arms up at her, "Go on, you, shoo!" After a few such
shouts from the hoomin, the owl screeched at him,
hissed, then took off across the field and into the darkness.

We stood up so the hoomin could see us. "Oh, I see
two intrepid detectives. Would you boys like a ride
and a key into the door?"

Baggins and I nodded emphatically. This kind
hoomin would not have been able to understand our
wordy responses, but nods are nearly universal gestures. He knelt on the ground and scooped Baggins
up into his cupped hands. "How about a ride in a
pocket?" he opened his jacket to reveal a spacious
compartment. Baggins dropped himself in and wiggled around till he was comfortable. The hoomin then
reached down for me. He very carefully put one hand
under my chest, and another under my butt. He held
me close to his chest, supporting my thumpers. This
guy knew how to handle a rabbit.

He carried us across the lot and over to the side door
we'd come out of. "OK, I need to put you down to get
the keycard out of my pocket." He knelt again, and set
me gently on the ground. Dromie sat in the entrance
of the recess, blocking the view of us from the outside.
Baggins scrambled out of the pocket, and we both
moved to sit at Dromie's front feet. Her hoomin dug
into his pocket and extracted his hotel key. The door
clicked, and he pulled it open. Baggins and I dashed
into the building and paused on the first step.

Dromie came over to us, "Are either of you hurt?"
I looked at Baggins. "I'm OK, ma'am."
Baggins patted himself a bit, "No troubles here,

thank you."

"Thank you very much, Miss Dromie, you and your hoomin have perfect timing."

"I'm just glad we were out for a walk when we were." She turned to her hoomin and relayed our thanks.

Now that we were in regular lighting, I could see that she was a lovely brindle color. I thanked the Universe for sending us such a kind and gentle helper.

She turned back to us. "My hoomin asks if you need any help getting back to your rooms?"

"No, ma'am, we can manage that. Thank you both so much!"

"You're both very welcome." She nuzzled us each in turn, and then trotted off down the ground floor hall with her hoomin.

We took the three flights of stairs slower than either of us would have liked to admit, pausing at each landing.

"What are you going to tell your hoomin?" Baggins asked.

"Same thing I always tell him, the truth."

"It won't worry him?"

"Of course it will, but he understands that risks have to be taken. No risk, no reward. Why? What are you going to tell your hoomin?"

"I might spare her the part about getting snuck up on by an owl."

"I don't know that she really did sneak up on us. She even let us know that she was close to us. I can't help wondering if she really would have attacked us."

"Oh, sure, it's easy to wonder that now that we're

safely inside. That thought may have occurred to you while we were out there, but I was busy trying to figure out how to not become dinner."

"You're right. I was focused on that, too. But there's nothing wrong with speculation, now that we are safe."

"True enough, and I'd rather do the speculating from a safe, warm hoomin snuggle."

I had to laugh. "Me too, Baggins, me too."

"So, how do we proceed in the morning?"

"We pick up where we left off. Visit each ferret booth, in turn, until we find our suspects."

"Before that, I think we had best check in with Shadow. See if he and his hoomin have heard anything from the officials."

"Good idea." We stopped outside Baggins' room door. It was propped open with the deadbolt. "Let's just plan to meet at Shadow's booth, first thing, then."

"Agreed. See you in the morning, Ears. Sleep well."

"See you then, good night, Baggins."

He wiggled himself through the gap in the door. I could hear his hoomin inside, "Baggins! Where have you been? I've been so worried…."

I made my way wearily down the hall to my room. My hoomin had the door propped open with my food bowl. I grabbed a pellet out of the bowl and hopped over it into the room. He scooped me up immediately. "Ears, buddy, are you OK?" He set me on the bed and helped me out of my coat. I chewed contentedly on the pellet while he fussed over me. He checked all over, making sure I wasn't hurt and pulled a few burrs from my fur. I purred while he combed out my fur, and rubbed my ears. Before too long, I was asleep.

Over breakfast, the next morning, I relayed our nighttime adventures to my hoomin. I could tell he was worried, but he hid it pretty well. He was openly grateful to Dromie and her hoomin, and vowed to find them to thank them personally.

"So what's the plan, today, then?" he asked.

"We'll start by checking in with Shadow, then visit each ferret booth until we find our suspects. Where we go from there will depend on circumstances, I think."

"Sounds like a good plan."

We finished our breakfast, and my hoomin packed himself a bag of granola and protein bars for lunch. I shrugged my coat on and stepped into my carrier. My hoomin closed my door, picked me up, and headed out the door. The trip across the field was, thankfully, uneventful.

A police officer checked us in at the door, and my hoomin walked straight back to our booth. He let me out of my carrier and picked me up for a snuggle.

"It's a quarter to nine, now. The show closes at noon," he told me. "If I'm going to be back to work tomorrow, it'd be best if we could leave no later than three. You think you could get this wrapped up before then?"

"We will do everything possible to solve it before we have to leave."

"And before Detective Campbell, no doubt."

"That too."

"Good luck, buddy." He set me on the floor, and I headed off to Shadow's booth.

I found Baggins under Shadow's back table, already talking to the fluffy feline.

"Ah, Ears, good. Shadow was just reporting that there is nothing new." He looked as well groomed as I must have. Apparently, his hoomin had also felt a need to employ a comb.

"I didn't expect them to get anything. I'd bet carrots their next move will be to search the hotel rooms."

"And vehicles, no doubt."

"My hoomin doesn't hold out much hope of them finding it," Shadow added, "he's convinced that the thief walked out with it before the lights even came back on."

"That's how a hoomin thief would have done it. Fortunately, we know it wasn't a hoomin," I nodded.

"At least not a hoomin who actually nicked it. The ferrets certainly must have delivered it to their hoomins," Baggins declared.

"I wonder how they fared at coming back to the hotel, last night?" I mused. I continued before anyone could offer an opinion or ask a question, "Anyway, we have eight booths to visit and only three hours. We should get busy."

Baggins had started to glare at me, then looked relieved when I redirected. "Yes, we should. Thank you, Shadow, we will let you know when we find your charm."

"Thank you both and good luck."

CHAPTER TWELVE

Jasper & Opal

◇◇◇◇◇◇◇

We decided to start in the far left aisle, just inside the front door. The plan was to go through the front-to-back aisles first, then the sideways aisles. It seemed daunting, but in reality, we only had eight booths to check. We would certainly get our walking in.

The first booth was occupied by two elder ferrets. They were curled up on the table, snuggled into battery heated beds. It seemed unlikely that they were our suspects, but looks can be deceiving. They welcomed us onto their table, and we could tell right away by their scent that they were not our suspects. We asked if they knew of any of their species who might commit the theft.

"Petty theft is a natural behavior for ferrets," the elder female told us, "but I can't imagine taking such a risk as that."

"No," her mate agreed. "I've never met another ferret that would be so bold as to steal a displayed item, in broad daylight, in the middle of a crowded building. A hoomin must have put them up to it."

"That's what the local police, believe, anyway," Baggins nodded.

We thanked the pair of elders and made our way to the next ferret booth. This one was down the central aisle, and it was occupied by three very young ferrets and their frazzled mother. Clearly not our suspects, but we still needed to find out if she had any information. The youngsters were about a third my size, and I distracted them by letting them wiggle around me, in and out of my coat, poking their noses into my pockets (I made sure to keep them out of the pocket occupied by my pop gun). It was very weird feeling them sniff across my back, but they were merely curious and playful. I never felt threatened, and they didn't scratch or bite. While I was playing with her babies, the mother answered Baggins' questions.

I only caught bits and pieces, but Baggins filled me in as we walked away. "She says she hasn't had a chance to meet any of the other ferrets here. Just like the oldsters, she couldn't think of a logical reason why any ferret would choose to steal such a thing on his own."

"So she thinks a hoomin put them up to it?"

"Yes. She also said that the police dog found a ferret scent at the scene. He and his handler hoomin were sent with the team to search the ferret booths."

"Wait!" I stopped Baggins and pulled him to the safety of a tablecloth. "The police know ferrets are involved?"

"Apparently so, according to what the police German Shepherd told her."

"Then how the thump do they not have suspects in custody?"

"No idea. Only reason she could figure, and I agree, is that Detective Campbell doesn't put any stock in what any animal detective or witness tells him."

"Well, that's stupid. Why have a dog on a search team, then?"

"No idea. I think, though, that we should mention the canine constable in future interviews, and see how the subjects react. It may give us one more tell if it makes someone particularly nervous."

"Agreed." I paused a moment, then shook my head. Why keep everyone here, if they had evidence to point to a specific suspect? I had to hope the rest of the interviews would turn up more clues.

Again, we skipped an aisle. We passed by Shadow's booth, but he was busy keeping an eye on browsers, so we didn't stop. The aisle furthest to the right, as one entered the building, had three ferret booths.

"Why must they spread everyone out like this?" Baggins moaned. "Wouldn't it make more sense to group similar species together?"

"From an investigative standpoint, sure, but the hoomins are here to sell things. If someone is looking for, say, hamster supplies, they would go to that section, get what they need, and leave. They would never see the offerings of anyone else. Then vendors like my hoomin, who sell things that are not species specific, would have much-reduced exposure, and thus fewer sales."

"Ah, I see. Mix them up, and people at the least have to walk past the other booths."

"Yup, and if they see something that catches their eyes, they might stop to ask questions. And if the vendor is any good at selling, questions can turn into sales."

Baggins nodded. "That does make sense. Oh well, I suppose walking is good for us."

I had to laugh. That was basically what I had already told myself.

The next booth on our map was a lone ferret. He was very shy, but friendly. It took a few assurances that we were not going to take him away from his hoomin for him to come out of his hide house. We hadn't yet seen one colored like him. His mask was a lighter brown than most, and his head and neck the color of heavy cream. All four of his paws were a silvery white. He introduced himself as Boots.

"I remember the big dog," Boots told us. "He was nice, but I was scared of him. I'm used to much smaller dogs."

"Being intimidating is a job requirement for police animals, that's why the Shepherds usually fill those ranks," I sympathized.

"Have you met any other ferrets here, Boots?" Baggins asked.

"No," Boots shook his head. "My hoomin is very protective of me. I don't like to get too far away from her."

"I understand," I smiled warmly. "Did the police dog say anything to you about the theft?"

"Yes, he said that he got the scent of a pair of ferrets and that he thought there were a male and a female."

I had suspected that, but didn't have enough experience with ferret scents to be confident in the distinction.

"Anything else?" Baggins asked.

"Yes, he was a bit upset that the hoomin in charge

was ignoring the clues he was providing. It seemed like he was feeling useless, like he was just there as a gesture, more than to actually help."

"Honestly," Baggins nodded, "I think he may be right about that."

"Can you think of anything else that might help us, Boots?"

The shy ferret thought for a moment. "No, I don't think so. Good luck, though."

"Thank you."

We bid Boots goodbye and moved on to the next set of suspects.

Getting the attention of this fourth booth's occupants was difficult. Their hoomin had arranged a large and elaborate setup for them. Tunnels, tubes, wheels, boxes, and a big box of what my hoomin called "packing peanuts" filled their pen. We counted three ferrets playing, and it took a couple minutes to get their attention. Finally, one popped up from the packing peanuts long enough to see that we were waiting. She called to the others, and they all bounced over to the front of the pen. There were actually five ferrets in this one pen. All were young and full of energy, but they were also quite polite.

"Have you all heard about the theft, yesterday?" I asked.

"Yes, that was naughty. No one should take and hide anything that can't be easily found or replaced." Keep in mind, here, that there were five eager critters all answering at once. I've taken the liberty of condensing them into more understandable responses.

"That's right," Baggins agreed. "Do you know of anyone who would be so naughty?"

"Well," they all looked to one of their own. "Billy, here, he took one of mommy's bracelets, once. She looked for it for a long time."

Billy's eyes got wide, and he backed himself up against the box, "But she did find it! She wasn't even really mad, just told me not to hide shiny metal things anymore! And I haven't! I didn't take the thing, yesterday!"

"It's OK, Billy," I assured him. "We aren't concerned about things you may have hidden in the past. We're looking for whoever took the charm, yesterday. That hasn't been found, yet."

"I didn't take it," Billy insisted, looking at his companions. They all shook their heads and asserted their innocence.

"Have any of you met any of the other ferrets, here?" Baggins redirected.

"We've seen a few others, but not talked to any."

"Did you all talk to the police dog, yesterday?"

"He was really nice. He asked to sniff each of us, then said he was sure none of us had done it."

"Did he say anything else?" Baggins asked.

"He agreed that it was really naughty to steal shiny metal. And he said that whoever had taken this piece of shiny metal would be put in major time-out for a long time."

It was pretty obvious these young ferrets didn't know anything helpful, so we bid them goodbye. They lost interest in us before we even left, and dove back into their packing peanuts.

"Is it just me, or is there a pattern here?" Baggins grumbled.

"Oh, you mean the one that apparently says ferret

parents don't socialize with other ferret parents?"

"Right. Or is it that ferrets are severely inattentive?"

"That, too, I think. I have to wonder if we're wasting our time with questions. Should we just stop long enough to sniff, then move on?"

"That's probably a good idea."

Baggins pulled the map out of his pocket. "We have one more booth in this aisle, then we move on to the crosswise rows."

"Perfect. I wonder, though, when we get there we should stop and ask Layla if she's heard anything new."

"Good idea."

The last ferret booth in this aisle was occupied by a pair of ferrets. Based on what I'd observed so far, these were a male and female pair. Both were completely black, with glittery guard hairs. Beautiful creatures, but their scents and answers to our standard questions told us they were definitely not our suspects.

On our way to the sixth ferret booth, Baggins suggested we take a detour to his hoomin's booth for a snack on the way to number seven. I agreed that that was an excellent idea, and thanked him for the offer.

This sixth booth was a ferret rescue, and the pen was subdivided into quarters. Each quarter held two to three ferrets, identified with names, pictures, and other pertinent adoption information. Baggins snuck around the back of the pen but returned shaking his head.

"I hope they can find their forever homes," I said as we walked on.

"Me too. They were all very polite about me sniffing around."

To get to Baggins' booth, we had to cross the entire-

ty of the cavernous room. Thankfully, we had gotten
the hang of avoiding hoomin feet. Then we had to
cross the shortcut gap. It wasn't as busy as it had been
yesterday, but we still had to time our sprint carefully.
Baggins stayed close to my side, and we were able to
stay together the whole way. I caught myself thinking
that I was going to miss the grumpy little guy.

Baggins' hoomin was closing a sale, as we got there.
As soon as the customer had left, Sue greeted us, "Hi,
boys. How's the investigation?"

While Baggins conversed with his hoomin, I took the
opportunity to stretch. Sue pulled a baggie out of her
apron pocket. She extracted three cookies and set two
in front of me, and one in front of Baggins. They were
hammy sized, so I was glad she gave me more than
one. They tasted like Timothy hay, banana, and cran-
berries. In other words, heavenly!

"Wow," I turned to Baggins, "these are amazing!
She makes these herself?"

"She does. In all sorts of flavors."

"Does she make bunny sized, too?"

"Yes, she does. She just didn't open one of those
bags, today."

"I'll have my hoomin buy some, then!"

After finishing our cookies, Baggins offered me some
water from his dish. Snack finished and washed down,
we waved goodbye to Sue and rounded the corner to
make our next stop. We paused at Layla's booth long
enough to ask her if she'd heard anything new. All
she had heard was how worried her hoomin was that
they would miss their flight home. We asked about the
police dog, and if he had said anything to her during
the search. All she had been told, and the questions

she had been asked, agreed with what others had told us. We knew we were on the right trail, and apparently, the police dog agreed. Why then were the hoomin investigators dragging their feet?

We thanked Layla and moved on to the eighth ferret booth. This was occupied by an exotic veterinarian selling supplements. The single ferret with him was an albino, completely white with bright ruby red eyes. He wanted to be helpful, but he wasn't able to tell us anything we hadn't already heard several times over.

Finally, with one booth left, we made our way back across the shortcut gap. Baggins' cynical side couldn't help bringing up that this one was probably going to be a bust, as well, and that the culprits must have slipped out during the initial confusion. I must admit, I was finding it difficult to stay optimistic.

The last ferret booth on our map was occupied by a middle-aged hoomin female. She had a cane next to her chair, and a clear tube running from her nose to a tall metal tank. The tank was tied to a wheeled dolly with a single handle. The animal occupants were a pair of ferrets. One was completely black, and the other had a very dark mask and feet. The scent hit us from across the aisle where we had been moving along the bottoms of the tablecloths. These were our suspects!

We ducked under the nearest table, realizing that we hadn't actually planned what to do when we found our suspects.

"OK, I was wrong," Baggins admitted, "there they are. Now what?"

"Let's take stock of what we see here."

"Right. The hoomin has an oxygen tank."

"And a cane."

"Yup. The ferrets are both in the pen."

"A short pen, too. I could hop over that easily."

"No doubt they could, too."

"Sure."

"So why are the hoomins not arresting them?" Baggins grumbled.

"I can think of two possible reasons. The most likely is that they don't have enough 'acceptable' evidence."

"Such as, they didn't find the charm when they searched?"

"Right."

"And the second reason?"

"Possibly trying to be over cautious about the hoomin's medical conditions? Don't want to overstress her and induce some kind of medical crisis? Seems pretty thin, but some hoomins are more sensitive about such things than others."

"Or maybe she's a local of good standing?"

"That's possible, too," I nodded.

"So, if you were a jewel thief, where would you hide the loot?" Baggins asked.

"Somewhere the cops wouldn't look."

"Or would at least hesitate to look."

"Like maybe somewhere that would be legally questionable to look," an idea was beginning to form in my head.

"Huh?"

"Medical devices are a touchy subject, and less likely to be thoroughly searched."

"Ah, so possibly in something related to the oxygen

tank?"

"That's what I'm starting to wonder."

"Blast!" Baggins hissed.

"What?"

"Here comes Detective I-don't-believe-animals-can-investigate-Campbell."

"Oh, pewps!"

The police detective and one uniformed officer stopped at our suspects' booth and started talking to the hoomin. The police dog was conspicuously missing. I glanced at Baggins.

"Let's go," he nodded.

We ran across the aisle to the front of the pen to question the ferrets. We asked their names, and the male introduced himself as Jasper and the female as Opal.

"We'd like to ask you both some questions," I told Jasper.

"Questions? About what?" Opal asked.

"About the theft, yesterday," Baggins answered.

"That's what the hoomin cops keep talking to our hoomin for. We can't give you any more answers than she can give them," Jasper smiled.

"We can't speak for the hoomin investigators, but we have been on your trail since the lights came back on yesterday."

"Our trail?" Opal actually batted her eyes.

"Yes, your trail!" Baggins lowered his tone authoritatively.

"You are mistaken, hamster, we were nowhere near that booth, yesterday." Jasper was beginning to get defensive.

"So, where were you when the lights went out, yesterday morning?" I asked.

"We were right here," Opal huffed.

"If you weren't near Shadow's booth, Jasper, why is your scent on the jewel case? Or the table next to it? Or the chair next to the table?"

I could see that Jasper was arguing with himself about how to respond. "I had gone there, earlier, to visit."

"Why that booth? The resident cat didn't recognize your scent, either."

"I like looking at sparkly things, and that cat and his hoomin have a lot of them."

"Uh huh." I turned to Opal. "And why was your scent on the wall leading up to the light switches?"

"What?" she acted indignantly. "I have no idea what you're talking about!"

"Well, then," Baggins interjected, "why were you in Petey the parrot's room the night before?"

"Parrot?" Jasper snorted. "Why would either of us go into a parrot's room?"

"I caught both your scents in his room. You hopped up on the chair, then on the table."

"That's ridiculous!" Opal exclaimed. I caught a bit of a nervous squeak in her voice, though.

"I ask again, hamster," Jasper hissed, "why would we go into a parrot's room? There's no reason for us to go into anyone's room but our own."

"You went in there," Baggins hissed back, "to steal his hoomin's diamond ring."

"Enough with the arguments, Jasper. Opal." I used my sternest tone. "Where is the ruby bird charm, and where is the diamond ring?"

"Yes, ferret!" Baggins and I whirled around at the voice that materialized behind us. Slinking toward us was the lovely white cat that had gotten me into this… Tabitha! She must have been watching. Biding her time, letting us do all the legwork. She continued, her voice dripping with contempt, "Where is *my* charm?"

Before anyone could respond, Jasper and Opal's hoomin started yelling at Detective Campbell. Baggins and I, concerned that we might get hurt in a scuffle, turned to watch the hoomins. A hiss from Tabitha drew my attention back to the ferrets, just in time to see Opal drop from the top of the pen and take off running.

CHAPTER THIRTEEN

The Chase

◇◇◇◇◇◇◇

I heard Baggins shout, "Go, Ears!"

I took off at a sprint. The ferrets had crossed the aisle and ducked under the nearest table. Their slender, slinky bodies made it easy for them to weave in and out between boxes and behind pens. I didn't bother diving in after them but was able to keep up from the aisle. Tabitha was right beside me, shouting unpleasantries at them. I saw Jasper slip through a small gap in the dividing wall, so I turned sharply to follow. I dove through the gap, moments after Opal, but they were already out of my reach. I leaped over a box and followed them into the next aisle. Seeing me still on their tails, Jasper lead Opal back under the booth tables, trying to lose me. I took half a second to realize that Tabitha was no longer running with me. She must not have been able to get through the gap in the wall.

Jasper looked over his shoulder to taunt me, "You'll never catch us, rabbit!"

When he turned back, he saw Tabitha at the end of the aisle. He swerved for another gap in the divider wall and slid through, Opal right behind him. I dove through the gap and nearly landed on both of them. They had run right into a metal pole and spent a fraction of a second reorienting themselves. I recognized the surprised squawk. They had run right into Petey's perch.

I took a gamble that Tabitha had made it back into this aisle and dashed off to the right. If we could sandwich them between us, we might have a chance. I didn't trust Tabitha any further than I could throw her, but I knew she wanted the charm just as much as any of us, so it seemed a reasonable risk to take. When one is small and adorable, however much of a tough guy one may be, it is still prudent to take help where one can get it.

Jasper and Opal emerged from under Petey's table, into the middle of the aisle. They turned away from me and came face to face with Tabitha. She growled at them, stopping them in their tracks. Jasper turned around, and I heard him tell Opal, "Back to mom." He stopped again when he saw me.

I'm not sure when I pulled out my pop gun, but it was in my paws, pointed right at Jasper. I had never used it before. Never even pulled it out of my pocket. Now here I was, all three pounds of my dwarf bunny self, pointing it at a pair (or was it a trio?) of predatory suspects.

Jasper hissed at me, and they turned to run across the aisle. Now under the tables, they started moving toward their own booth. I shoved the pop gun back into my pocket as I ran after them.

Tabitha pulled up beside me, "Nice try."

"Yeah, sure." I glanced over at her and noticed Petey had flown up to the top of the divider wall, and was following discreetly.

Up ahead, I could see that Detective Campbell was still questioning the hoomin suspect. If he had even noticed the ferrets escaping, he hadn't let it distract him. I had to admit I was impressed by that, especially since them dashing off must have been intended as a distraction. It was distracting. Every dog they had run past was barking, and several hoomins were shouting, as well. No doubt everyone in the building was wondering what all the commotion was about.

Jasper and Opal's hoomin had been paying close attention to where her critters were. It was clear she was waiting for them to return, as she bent in her chair to let them jump into her arms. Tabitha tried to jump after them, but I hopped into her side, throwing off her trajectory. She landed awkwardly under the table and slid into a box.

The ferrets' hoomin picked up her cane and was using it to block Tabitha's new approach. She even took a swing at me, but I was already heading over to where Baggins was.

"Here, Ears! I've got Shadow's scent on the oxygen tank." He pointed at the black plastic base. Before I could say anything, his eyes got wide, and he shouted, "DUCK!"

I flattened myself against the floor and felt the cane whoosh over my head. Pushing off with my thumpers, I lunged to the side, and behind the tank. Baggins had squeezed himself into the pen, and dove under a play tube. The hoomin kept coming at me, swinging the cane. I dashed right and left, staying just out of range of the swinging club. I watched as she got her feet more and more tangled in the air hose.

Before she could recover, she started to trip. She re-directed her fall back toward the chair, pulling the hose tight. Time slowed as I watched her fall back. The hose, attached to the top of the tank, started pulling the tank over. She missed the chair and landed on her fanny on the floor. The oxygen tank impacted the floor with a clang. The plastic base cracked and popped off the tank. I'll admit I had always wondered if the bottoms of those tanks were flat. Turns out, this one at least is rounded like half of a ball.

Only slightly more interesting were the two sparkly treasures that spilled out of the tank's base. One gold and diamond ring and one ruby encrusted Scarlet Bird.

CHAPTER FOURTEEN

Arrested

◇◇◇◇◇◇

No one moved, we all just stared at the jewels in stunned silence. Detective Campbell broke the trance, "Ma'am, I'm placing you under arrest for theft...."

Before he could say anything else, Tabitha pounced on the gems, picked up the bird in her mouf, and sprung away. As I jumped over the tank to chase after her, I felt a weight on my coat.

"Keep going," Baggins shouted as he crawled up my coat onto my back. "Don't let her get away!"

I sprinted to catch up as Tabitha rounded the nearest corner and turned toward the front door. She turned again, headed up the aisle toward Baggins' booth. Somehow, I was closing the gap between us, but I could feel a twinge in the leg I'd hurt the previous summer. I tried to ignore it, determined to get the charm back, and not have to go back to the vet.

Tabitha turned left and ran down the central aisle, apparently headed for the door. With a straight path, she picked up speed, and I started falling behind. I let out a growling scream and pushed myself faster.

About halfway down the aisle, a green bomb dropped down on Tabitha. Petey had slammed into her back, knocking her sprawling. The charm bounced away from her as she flipped over to swat at her feathered attacker. Avoiding the claws, Petey flapped up onto the nearest table.

Tabitha looked around and saw where the charm had come to rest. She leaped toward it but was stopped mid-air by a large ball of black fluff. Shadow had been drawn by the commotion and intercepted her.

"Ears, the charm!" Baggins shouted from behind my head.

"Right!" I pushed off with my thumpers and landed right next to the jewel. I picked it up in my mouf, and took off straight toward my hoomin's booth. I had seen a gap in the divider wall, before, and was now sure I could get through it. Baggins saw where I was headed, and flattened against my back.

I jumped high through the gap, slipping through easily, and landed on a box on the other side. I let my thumpers slide across the top of the box, then pushed off when I felt the edge. It wasn't perfectly graceful. The box was empty, so it flew back as I pushed against the edge, but it was enough to keep me from stumbling when I landed on the floor.

We came out into the open aisle exactly where I wanted to be, just to the left of my hoomin's booth. He was standing in front of the table, and dropped to his knees when he saw us headed for him. I jumped into his waiting arms and snuggled close to his chest. I felt Baggins let out a relieved sigh.

"That'll do, rabbit, that'll do," Baggins whispered,

patting my head.

My hoomin had started walking as soon as he had
hold of us. He walked as quickly as he could toward
the far corner and Jasper and Opal's booth. We met
Detective Campbell at the shortcut gap.

"Detective," my hoomin called out, "Ears has the
charm for you."

"Good." Campbell held out his hand under my chin,
and I dropped the Scarlet Bird into his palm.

"Baggins?" Sue was coming up behind my hoomin,
and she sounded worried.

"He's here," my hoomin turned to her.

"Oh, thank god!" She stroked my head once, then
lifted Baggins off my back. "Thank you, Ears, for keeping my little guy safe."

I was too exhausted, so I just wiggled my nose in
response.

"Officer," a new female hoomin's voice called from
behind the detective. "My cat was just attacked by two
animals. I want them arrested!"

Campbell turned around, and we saw Tabitha in
her hoomin's arms. I looked her over, and aside from
some ruffled fur, she seemed unhurt.

"And who are you?" Campbell asked.

"I think Ears and I can answer that," my hoomin
spoke up.

"Alright, please do."

"That cat came by, yesterday morning, to talk to
Ears." My hoomin let me rearrange in his arms, so I
could explain and he could translate. "He's saying that
she wanted to hire him to retrieve a piece of jewelry
that had been stolen from her. She lead him to the

jeweler's booth, and pointed out the ruby bird that was in the case."

"This ruby bird?" Campbell asked, holding up the charm.

"Yes, that one. Ears was immediately suspicious. I mean, naturally, right? What kind of nut case would prominently display a stolen item?"

"A complete cabbage!" Baggins and I both declared. Our hoomins looked at us, then at each other, then laughed.

"What? What'd they say?" Campbell was confused.

"They answered the question. Only a 'complete cabbage' would display a stolen item."

"Cabbage?"

"A British slang term for idiot," Sue explained.

"Oh, right." Campbell shook his head. "Anyway, I think this would be a good time for all of us to go talk to the charm's actual owner. Please, all of you, come with me."

With Detective Campbell leading the way, and his officers herding from behind, we all walked over to Shadow's booth.

As we walked down the aisle toward Shadow's booth, we heard an announcement over the public address system that it was twelve noon, and the pet expo was closing. Security guards were walking around, asking visitors to please conclude their current purchases and head for the exit. Those three hours seemed to have flown by, but my body felt like I had been running for a lot longer than that. I was really starting to look forward to a salad, sleep, and a nice long snuggle.

Shadow was watching as his hoomin finished the

transaction with his last customer. When he saw all of us coming, he growled at Tabitha. That drew his hoomin's attention.

"Ah, Detective Campbell. Any luck?" the jeweler asked.

"Yes indeed, Mr Merritt," Campbell held up the charm.

"Oh, thank heaven! So who…." He stopped when he saw Tabitha and her hoomin. "Well, what do you know. Gabby Wilson, I should have known it was you!"

We all looked from Mr Merritt to Tabitha's hoomin.

"It wasn't me, and it wasn't Tabitha!" she declared.

"You know this woman, Mr Merritt?" Campbell asked.

"Yes, sir. She's what you might call a rising star in the jewel thief community."

"You've been out of the game too long, Frank." The contempt in her voice was thick enough to cut with a knife.

"I tired of the game, Gabby. It's far easier, and safer, to make the pretties than to steal them."

"Why did you not tell me of her, yesterday, Mr Merritt?" Campbell asked.

"To be completely honest, Detective, I didn't know she was here."

Campbell turned to Tabitha and Gabby. "Were you planning on stealing this charm, Miss Wilson?"

"Of course! That rag mop," she gestured to Shadow, "doesn't deserve it. Why should he get all the beautiful things?"

"Oh, for cats' sake, Gabby! Why not just buy something for Tabitha?" Mr Merritt asked, exasperated.

"At your prices?" she spat. "What kind of jewel thief would I be if I couldn't just take it?"

I happened to see Detective Campbell roll his eyes. "And what about you, ma'am," he turned to Jasper and Opal's hoomin. "Why did you have your ferrets take it?"

"Who would suspect ferrets of stealing anything? People steal, not animals." She replied flatly.

"So, no personal motives against either of these two?" he gestured at Mr Merritt and Miss Wilson.

The lady holding the ferrets in their carrier in one hand, and her cane in the other shrugged. "No, never seen either of them before."

Campbell held up the diamond ring. "And what about this? Where did they pinch this from?"

"Oh, Baggins can explain that," Sue spoke up. Baggins was sitting on her right shoulder.

"Great, please do," Campbell nodded.

"It belongs to a lady, Mary Harrison. She makes toys and treats for parrots…." Sue turned to gesture toward Petey's booth, and we saw that she was walking toward us. Petey was perched on her left shoulder.

"Yes, sorry I didn't report it missing." Miss Harrison said. "I honestly thought Petey had stashed it somewhere. He insisted that he didn't, and went to see Mr Baggins about it."

"So you confirm that this is your ring, Miss Harrison?" Campbell asked, holding the ring up for her to see.

"Definitely! I inherited it from my grandmother."

"Thank you. I will need to log it as evidence, though."

"Of course, I understand."

"Good," Campbell paused and looked over all of us.
"Now, the show is closed, and the visitors are gone. I
need all of you, animals included, to come down to the
station with me. I need written statements from everyone. Especially our two private detectives."

We all agreed. Campbell asked his officers to take
Miss Wilson back to her booth for Tabitha's carrier and
informed her that she was under arrest. I was surprised that she didn't argue. My hoomin, Baggins and
Sue, and Mary and Petey all walked back to our respec-
tive booths for our carriers.

"I bet you're hungry, aren't you, buddy?" my hoomin asked me.

"Very. Thirsty, too."

He grabbed a handful of hay and shoved it to the
back of my carrier, then grabbed my water bottle and
collapsible bowl. "I'll have to wait to give you water
until we get there," he said as I stepped into the carrier.

"Sure," I said, grabbing a mouthful of hay.

CHAPTER FIFTEEN

Police Interrogations

◇◇◇◇◇◇◇

Detective Campbell put Baggins and me and our hoomins in an interrogation room with a pad of statement forms each. Since the animal's side of the conversations with their hoomins is telepathic, we would not be interfering with each other. Petey and his hoomin were taken to a lounge area where they could write their statement.

My hoomin is no slouch when it comes to writing. He has done plenty of technical writing, but that is very different than the sort of writing needed for a formal police statement. This was more formal than my usual editor does, but she would have been much easier to dictate to for this. Oh well.

When we were finished, Campbell came back in and asked us to tell him about our investigation. That may seem odd, why not just read the statements? Thing is, sometimes telling brings up details that may not have been remembered during the writing. It was an advanced investigation strategy, and I had to be even more impressed with Detective Campbell.

I turned to my hoomin. "Detective," my hoomin asked, "before we get started, Ears would like to ask a question?"

"Sure."

"When you were questioning us, you seemed rather dismissive of what he and Baggins had already learned. Why now are you seemingly so open to what they have to say?"

"Well, to be frank, I've never experienced this 'hoomin-in-pet bond'. I really don't have a problem with Pet PIs, but I prefer to conduct my investigation without their clues clouding my thinking."

I nodded and continued through my hoomin. "What about the police dog? We heard from every ferret we talked to that he had caught a ferret's scent at the scene, yet they all got the impression that you were ignoring that evidence."

"The scent may have been at the scene, but they may also have handed it off to another animal. I had to take that information with the proverbial grain of salt until I knew more. What made you boys so sure it was ferrets?"

We told him the whole thing from the beginning. He chuckled when we told him about the sheep and their furry snakes. After admitting to losing the scent and hunting for a map, he held up a hand to stop us.

"I take it that's about the time I sent everyone back to their booths?"

"Yes, that's right."

He wrote a note in his folder. "OK, please continue."

We went on and told him about visiting Petey's room and following a fresh scent down the stairs.

"Why on earth would you go outside at night?"

"I had the idea that they might be off to hide the jewelry somewhere," Baggins explained.

"That was a reasonable assumption. We had them under surveillance, but they didn't lead to anything. Please continue."

We told him about the trip across the field, the insanity of the carnival, and the harrowing trip back. After describing our narrow escape from the owl, my hoomin said that he'd like to thank Dromie and her hoomin personally. Sue and Baggins agreed.

Campbell flipped back through his notes for a minute. "There are no Great Danes in the vendor lists." He flipped a few more pages. "And none registered at the hotel, either."

Baggins and I described Dromie with as much detail as we could, but Detective Campbell was sure they hadn't questioned anyone with a Great Dane. I remembered something my great grandpa had written in his diary, "Oftentimes, the solving of one mystery presents another." I shook my head and shrugged. We may never know who our saviors were, where they came from, or where they went.

Campbell nodded through our description of our morning investigations. He nodded as he jotted a few more notes into his folder. "I was glad you boys came up to question the ferrets. I would have helped with the chase, but I needed to keep the human there."

"Sure, we understand," Baggins mumbled.

Detective Campbell smiled, and looked at all four of us, in turn. "I wonder if you folks would be willing to assist with the interrogations of the others?"

My hoomin was surprised at that. "That seems odd, don't you have police animals for that?"

"We have dogs, sure, but they are sometimes too intimidating. Ears and Baggins seem very capable, and since they have first-hand knowledge of this case, I think they will be able to get more out of them than a Shepherd would."

Baggins and I looked at each other and shrugged. We turned to Campbell and nodded. He may not be able to hear us, but some gestures are universal enough. Campbell smiled, closed his folder, and stood.

"Great. We'll start with the ferrets and their human."

Jasper and Opal were on harnesses and leashes. Their hoomin was handcuffed to the table. Detective Campbell sat on the far side of the table and gestured to us to fill the other two seats, facing the suspects.

"For the record, ma'am, I've read you your rights?" Campbell asked.

"Yes. Who are they?" she rolled her head in our direction.

"This here is Detective Ears O'Fluffin, Pet Private Investigator, and his human, Scott. And the hamster is Detective Baggins, of the British Pet Detection Service, and his human, Sue."

Jasper glared at Baggins, and his hoomin rolled her eyes. "Never heard of animal detectives, before," she sneered.

"Let's start with your name, ma'am," Campbell continued.

"Hattie Brixton. And this is Jasper and Opal."

"And you admit to instructing your ferrets to steal the ruby collar charm?"

"No."

"No?" Campbell looked up from his notebook.

"I didn't tell them to take that, specifically, just to take something pretty."

"And what about Miss Harrison's diamond ring? Did you instruct them to steal something from a hotel guest?"

"I told them to have some fun. I wasn't surprised they came back with a ring, but I wasn't going to discourage them from keeping in practice."

"Uh huh," Campbell flipped a few pages in his folder. "And what about the oxygen tank? Our lab reports that it's empty."

"Full tanks are heavy, detective. An empty one is easier to move around."

"So you don't actually need the oxygen?"

"No."

I had noticed that she didn't have the tube in her nose, anymore.

"So why lug it around?" Campbell continued.

"The base is a good place to hide small items. People don't like to search medical equipment."

"Any other reason?"

Miss Brixton sighed. "How many people would suspect someone with a cane and oxygen tank of being a thief? Really, Detective, how many more stupid questions are you going to ask?"

Campbell smiled and turned to me. He nodded once, and I took that as a cue to question the ferrets.

I looked at Jasper. "Why do you steal for your hoomin?"

"Why do you think, rabbit?" he tried to make the word "rabbit" into an insult.

I smiled at him and turned to Opal. "What made you decide to steal the ruby charm, Opal?"

"It's really pretty, and we thought mom would be able to sell it and get lots of money for it," she replied cheerfully.

Jasper huffed a sigh and rolled his eyes.

"Do you always steal when your mom tells you to, Opal?" Baggins asked.

"Well, yeah," she looked at me then back at Baggins. "It makes her happy to see the sparkly things we bring her. And it's fun to figure out how to do it without getting caught."

I relayed this information to my hoomin, and he told Campbell.

Campbell turned to Miss Brixton. "Why ferrets?"

She looked up at the ceiling and sighed. "Because they are small and can get into tight places," she said, her tone like she was explaining to a child. "They're fast and smart, and don't leave fingerprints."

Baggins and I looked at each other, then laughed.

"Maybe not fingerprints," I told her through my hoomin, "but their scents are just as unique."

"Cops don't dust for scent, rabbit."

Since when did "rabbit" become an insult? I was starting to think these three belonged in a loony bin.

"Why do you think they have police dogs?" my hoomin translated. "The hoomin cops may not be able to pick up scents, but the dogs can."

"Whatever," she sneered.

"One last question, Miss Brixton," Campbell redirected. "Do you know Miss Gabrielle Wilson, and her cat, Tabitha?"

"Never heard of them."

Campbell pulled out a pair of photos and slid them across the table. "This is Miss Wilson and Tabitha."

"I saw them at the expo, today, but I don't know them."

"You're certain?"

"Yes, I'm sure."

"Thank you." Campbell stuffed the photos back in his folder and closed it. "The officer will come in and move you and your critters into a holding cell." He stood and gestured to us to exit the room.

We left the room with Campbell and followed him into a break room. He set his notebook on a table and turned to us. "Mr Merritt, Shadow's human, confirmed what Shadow had told you boys about where the ruby charm came from. He also explained that he barely knew Tabitha's human. We took Mr Merritt's statement and let him return to the hotel."

Campbell gestured us to chairs and offered our hoomins coffee. My hoomin set me on the table and pulled a baggy of pellets out of his pocket. He opened the pouch and transferred a handful of pellets onto the table in front of me. Sue had a similar bag for Baggins and left him a small pile of pellets to munch on. Detective Campbell returned to the table with three coffee mugs, then went back to the counter. He sat and handed out two cups of cold water for me and Baggins. He may not have experienced the hoomin-pet bond, but he was a gracious host.

"Our next step is to question Miss Wilson and Tabitha," Campbell explained. "It seems that you two believe that they were not involved in the actual theft, is that right?" he asked Baggins and me.

"That's right," I said through my hoomin.

"Correct," Baggins agreed through Sue.

"I'm waiting to hear back from a few sources..."
Campbell stopped as a uniformed officer came in and
handed him a manila folder. He opened the folder and
scanned through the three pages it contained. "Ah,
yes, I thought so." He closed the folder and looked at
us. "Turns out that Miss Wilson and Tabitha are both
wanted in two other states for involvement in unrelat-
ed thefts."

This news wasn't surprising, and we all nodded.

"Once we're sure there was no collusion between
Tabitha and the ferrets, I'll call the authorities from the
other states. They can argue over who gets her first."

Coffee and snacks finished, Campbell lead us into
a third interrogation room. Tabitha was loafed on
the table in front of her hoomin, wearing a harness
and leash, and clearly unhappy about the restraint.
Tabitha's hoomin was handcuffed to the table.

We sat across from the suspects, as we had before.
Detective Campbell opened his folder, and flipped
through his notes, letting the silence draw out.

Miss Wilson finally broke the silence, "We did not
steal that charm, and we had nothing to do with those
that did."

"But you were going to?" Campbell asked.

She shrugged. "Not that one, specifically, that was
Tabitha's choice."

"So why did she go to Detective O'Fluffin?"

"I suggested she try to find someone else to take
something. That black rag mop would have recognized Tabitha, and Merritt would have recognized me.
It made more sense to use a patsy."

"That's sound reasoning, Miss Wilson. But why a

PPI?"

Miss Wilson looked to Tabitha. "Apparently," Miss Wilson translated, "she thought he would be less likely to be suspected. And, if he did get nabbed for it, that'd be one less PPI out there."

"Why steal something at the expo, at all?"

"Tabitha wanted a charm for her collar. I couldn't afford one, and certainly didn't know how to make one, so that left one option."

"Why would Tabitha want to take something from someone who would recognize her?"

Miss Wilson translated for Tabitha, "Because I deserve it. I deserve the best. What has Shadow done to deserve such fancy things? Nothing! Other cats get all these luxurious beds and jewelry. When they get that stuff, I don't get any. I deserve more than they do!"

Campbell thought for a moment.

"Baggins has a question for Tabitha," Sue spoke up.

"Go ahead," Campbell nodded.

"Why do you think that they deserve less?" Baggins asked through Sue.

"I suffered more!" Tabitha growled, and her hoomin translated. "Shadow was pampered, compared to how I was treated. Especially as his coloring evened out."

Miss Wilson looked embarrassed. "Since I got Tabitha, I've been stealing less. Last time I was in prison, I learned how to knit. I made a few things for her after I got her. She seems to appreciate them, but they are a far cry from a silk velvet pillow and diamond encrusted collars."

"Some would think the handmade items far better than what can be bought in a store," I explained through my hoomin.

Tabitha started purring as Miss Wilson stroked her back. "Anyway," Miss Wilson continued, "what few friends I have, saw what I'd made, and offered to buy some for their cats. They told others, and before long I had a decent customer base. I started doing pet shows last year. I don't make much, but so far I have been able to pay for the booths with a little to spare."

"Getting established is a slow process." My hoomin nodded. "Especially for handmade art stuffs. I didn't really start making much until I found a decent printer for the smaller things like note cards."

Sue nodded in agreement.

"I think…" Miss Wilson said wistfully, "I think I'd like to give up the thief thing. If my knit stuff would take off, I wouldn't need to, anyway. And I see how happy Merritt is."

"I'm glad to hear that, Miss Wilson," Campbell said. "A search did turn up two outstanding warrants, and I will be calling those states."

"I understand that. Will I be able to keep Tabitha with me?"

"Most likely. She is listed on the warrants, as well. Most judges like to keep prisoners' animals with them."

"Good."

Campbell looked to us, but neither Baggins nor I had any more questions.

"Thank you, Miss Wilson. The officer will come to take you and Tabitha to the holding cells."

We followed Campbell out of the room and over to his desk.

"So," Baggins asked through his hoomin, "Shadow won't be getting his charm back for a while, then?"

"No, it will be held as evidence until the trial is over." Campbell fished through a file box on his desk.

"And what about Petey's hoomin's ring?" Baggins asked.

"Well," Campbell opened a small plastic evidence bag. "I talked to Petey's hoomin, and she has decided not to press charges. She believed Miss Brixton when she said the ferrets took it on their own, and she didn't think it was right to punish her for their very ferret like behavior." Campbell turned the bag upside down and let the diamond ring drop into his palm. "So I'll give it to you, and you can return it to your client." He held the ring out so Baggins could take it.

"Ah, thank you, Detective," Sue translated as Baggins picked up the ring in both paws. "You are a hamster among men."

Campbell's face took on a quizzical look.

Sue chuckled, "He means that as a compliment."

"Sure, uh, thanks."

We all had a laugh.

"Come on, I'll show you all out," Campbell lead us down the elevator and out the front door of the precinct building.

Our hoomins kept Baggins and me out, bringing our carriers along. There was an officer standing next to his squad car, waiting for us. It was a beautiful summer evening, and the birds were singing their twilight songs.

"I want to thank you all for your help in this case." Campbell looked to each of us. "I know it didn't seem like it, at first, but I had to follow my own investigative procedure."

"We understand," I assured through my hoomin.

"Absolutely," Baggins added.

"Well, if you're ever in the area again, drop me a line," Campbell handed our hoomins each a business card.

"We will," my hoomin smiled.

"I hope we can come back, next year," Sue said. "It's a long trip, but I made a lot of sales. And Baggins had a grand adventure."

Detective Campbell walked us to the waiting police car and helped our hoomins manage our carriers as we hopped in for the drive back to the hotel. Before our hoomins closed us in, Baggins and I waved goodbye to our official hoomin counterpart. He waved back as we drove away.

CHAPTER SIXTEEN

Saying Goodbye

◇◇◇◇◇◇◇

Six of us filled the largest table on the patio of the hotel's restaurant. Baggins sat on the table next to his hoomin's plate, munching pellets and yogurt drops. I was in my hoomin's lap, my salad plate on the table where I could reach it. Petey perched on his hoomin's shoulder. She would hand him bits of fruit from a bowl next to her plate. The bright, cool morning was perfect for eating outside, and we all were enjoying the slight breeze and warm sunshine.

"When does your flight leave, Sue?" Petey's hoomin asked.

"Two o'clock, but we need to be there around eleven."

"I can imagine security and Customs will be a nightmare," my hoomin said.

"Well, I was able to sell a little more than half of what I came with, so it won't be quite as bad this time."

"Wow," Petey's hoomin's eyes got wide. "You did really well, then!"

"I did. It was definitely worth the trip. How did you

do, Scott?"

"Not bad," my hoomin nodded. "Sold three big pieces, all of the note card packs, and about half of the matted prints."

"Any commissions?" Petey's hoomin asked.

"Two. Less than I'd hoped, but much better than none."

"Oh," Baggins said as he reached into his hoomin's shirt pocket. He pulled out the ring and walked across the table to Petey. "Since your hoomin isn't pressing charges, I'm able to return this to you and your hoomin." He held the ring out to Petey.

"Thank you so much, Detective Baggins!" Petey whistled. He took the ring in his beak, turned it around a few times with his tongue, then held it out for his hoomin to take.

Miss Harrison took the ring from Petey and slipped it on her finger. She snuggled Petey against her cheek, "Sorry I blamed you, sweetie." She looked at Baggins, "What do we owe you?"

Baggins laughed and shook his head. "Nothing," Sue translated. "I wouldn't be able to take it on the plane, and I think this adventure has been enough of a reward."

"Aw, I'm glad you had a good time." Miss Harrison held out her finger to shake Baggins' paw.

After breakfast, Baggins and I went with our hoomins back to the expo hall to pack everything up. I was checking that my carrot juice bottle was tightly closed when I heard Sue's voice.

"We brought something for Ears," she said.

"Oh?" my hoomin asked.

She handed him three bags of bunny cookies. "Here, and here's my contact information."

"Wow, we can't take all this, let me pay you for them."

"No, no," she insisted. "There were only those three left in the box, and they won't fit in any of the others. Not having to take them through the airport is payment enough."

"Fair enough," my hoomin laughed. "Oh, and I have something for you and Baggins." My hoomin opened his portfolio folder. "I sketched it, yesterday, and added some color last night." He handed her a piece of paper from his sketchbook.

Sue took it gingerly. "Oh, wow. That's so perfect!"

I had seen it last night. It was a portrait of me and Baggins. In it, I'm holding the Scarlet Bird while Baggins and I admire it. It was nice for a quick sketch, and not embarrassing at all.

"Thank you, so much!"

"You're most welcome. Here's my card, so you have my contact info."

Baggins popped out of Sue's pocket. She pulled him out and set him on the ground at her feet. He came over to me and smiled.

"Shadow is at his booth, minding the shop while his hoomin takes boxes out to their van. I thought you and I ought to go talk to him."

"Good idea." I turned to let my hoomin know where we were going.

"Sure, buddy. I'm gonna run a load out, myself."

I nodded, and Baggins and I set off for Shadow's corner booth. The walk gave us a chance to talk.

"I'm glad you were here, this weekend, Baggins. I

don't think I could have gotten through this case without your help."

"Neither of us could have done it alone. I'm pretty sure I owe you my life a few times over."

"Once, anyway," I chuckled. "We both owe Dromie, whoever she was."

"It seems one of us has a guardian angel."

"Probably yours. I have my great grandpa."

"Oh?"

"He's the reason I'm a detective, and he helped me find my hoomin."

"Oh yes, I remember that story, now. That was your Halloween story for Bunnyzine, yes?"

"That's the one. He also helped us find a guidebook."

"I had wondered where that had dropped from. Well, thank you, Great Grandpa."

"And thank you, Dromie."

"Detectives!" Shadow trotted over to greet us. "I'm so glad you came over. I was about to come looking for you."

"We thought you'd like to hear the results of yesterday's interrogations," Baggins smiled.

"Yes, please!"

"Tabitha and her hoomin are wanted in two other states, so they are being held for one of those authorities to pick her up," Baggins explained.

"The two ferrets and their hoomin will be tried here for the theft of your charm," I continued. "Unfortunately, that means that the police will have to keep your charm as evidence until the trial is over."

Shadow nodded. "My hoomin explained that. We

will also have to come back for the trial, though we don't know when that will be."

"Hopefully, it will be a short one," Baggins nodded.

"What about Petey, did his hoomin get her ring back, or are they keeping that, too?"

"Petey's hoomin decided not to press charges for that, so she has her ring back," Baggins explained.

"Good, good." Shadow paused. "I have something for each of you. You both did so much to help me, that it doesn't seem right you don't get a fee of some sort."

"That's not necessary," Baggins and I tried to protest.

"No, no, it is necessary. Baggins, I know taking foodstuffs on an international flight is complicated, so my hoomin and I decided on a non-food payment. Wait here, please." Shadow trotted back to his carrier and disappeared inside.

I looked at Baggins. He shrugged, then gestured a question at me. I shrugged in response.

Shadow returned carrying two packages wrapped in green tissue paper and tied with narrow silk ribbon. He set them on the floor in front of us and pushed one toward Baggins, and the other toward me. The packages had our names neatly printed on them with silver ink. Each package was about an inch and a half square, with a slight bulge in the middle.

"Have your hoomins open them for you," Shadow explained. "There's a slip of paper with care instructions included."

Baggins and I looked at each other, both silently asking the same question: What could possibly be in these packages that required care instructions?

"Thank you, Shadow," I carefully slipped the package in my pocket.

Baggins slid his inside his vest and zipped it closed
to hold it. "Thank you, very much."

"No, thank you!" Shadow insisted. "Thank you both
so very much." He lowered his head, and we each
pressed our foreheads against his.

"Shadow," his hoomin called as he walked over to
us. "We're ready to go, did they get their packages?"

We all nodded.

Mr Merritt knelt on the floor next to Shadow and
held out a finger for me to shake, then to Baggins.
"Thank you, both. Safe travels."

Baggins and I waved goodbye to Shadow and Mr
Merritt, as they headed to the front door.

When we got back to my hoomin's booth, we found
both our hoomins waiting for us and talking. Both
were ready with their last loads. Baggins and I pulled
our packages out and handed them to our hoomins.
We were picked up, and set on the table to watch while
they unwrapped the small bundles. Under the tissue
paper was a small plastic baggy. Inside the baggy was
a folded piece of paper and a sparkling silver charm.
Mine was a capital letter E, and Baggins' was a capital
B. They were set with tiny colorless gemstones. The
letters were a little bigger than half an inch tall and
designed to hang from a collar ring.

My hoomin unfolded the paper, and read it aloud,
"Genuine diamonds set in white gold. Buff regularly
with a soft cloth."

Wow, real diamonds! Set in something that won't
tarnish like silver. Baggins and I looked at each other,
gaping at the shocking value of the fees that we never
asked for. I plopped down on my cotton bottom and

studied the charm, not sure what to say.

"Blimey," Baggins whispered.

"Well said," I agreed.

"Not bad for two days of work, huh, buddy?" my hoomin asked, petting my head.

"Mr Merritt is very generous," Sue agreed. She pulled in and let out a deep sigh. "Well, Baggins, we'd best be off to the airport."

He nodded and stuffed his charm in his vest pocket. I dropped mine into my inside coat pocket and stood to say goodbye.

Baggins held out his paw, and I took it in both of mine. "Well, Ears, I must bid you adieu."

"Be well, Baggins." I knew, at this moment, that I was really going to miss him.

"Make sure your hoomin stays in touch with mine."

"I don't intend to let him forget. Have a safe flight."

"And you a safe drive."

With one last paw squeeze, Baggins turned and walked into his blanket lined carrier. Sue swung her last bag onto her shoulder and picked up the carrier with the same hand. She held out her hand, and my hoomin shook it. We waved goodbye as they walked out the front door.

CHAPTER SEVENTEEN

And Home Again

◇◇◇◇◇◇◇

I plopped my poof onto the white tablecloth, staring at the front door, while my hoomin picked my carrier off the floor and set it on the table.

"You're gonna miss him, aren't you?" my hoomin asked.

"Yeah, I will. I guess working with a partner isn't so bad, after all."

"Well, I think Baggins is one of a kind. Don't expect to find another like him."

"I know, and I don't."

"Should we head back to the hotel, and pack up there?"

"Yeah," I sighed. I stood up and walked slowly into my carrier.

My hotel room pen had already been packed, so my hoomin just had to gather his stuff. He had set my carrier on the bed and opened the door. I shrugged off my coat and folded it carefully, making sure the diamond charm wouldn't fall out. On the bed, I worked through my whole stretching routine. Cozy as my basket on the passenger seat was, there wasn't room to stretch out, and three hours was a long time. When I was done, I flopped on one of the pillows. I had needed a good flop all weekend but hadn't had the time.

I must have fallen asleep because I didn't hear my hoomin take his suitcase out to the car. He woke me up with a soft pet from my nose to my pouf.

"Ready to go, buddy?"

I took a deep breath and shook off the sleepiness. "Yeah, let's go home."

I sat up in my basket, staring out the window. My hoomin was listening to a book on CD. Something about computers that made no sense to me, so I let my mind wander. Thinking back to other cases I'd submitted for the readers of Bunnyzine, I figured they would likely enjoy this one. I decided to have my hoomin contact my editor, when we got home. She is one of those very rare hoomins that can hear animals without a hoomin/pet bond. Good thing, too, since my hoomin barely has time for his art, never mind transposing my scribblings.

"What ya thinking about, buddy?" my hoomin asked. I hadn't heard the speakers go silent.

"Oh, just wondering how many issues it would take to relay this case to Bunnyzine."

"Most of your cases that you've told took place over a few hours. This one was two and a half days."

"Yeah, so?"

"This is probably more of a book, than a short story."

I thought about that for a few minutes. Can a detective be an author, too?

"Could you email my editor when we get home?" I

asked.

"Of course!"

I settled into a loaf, thinking about what might be
involved in writing a book. I must have fallen asleep
because I suddenly felt like I was floating. My hoomin
was carrying my basket, with me in it, into the house. I
hopped out, stretched, and flopped on my bed. There
wasn't anything I could do to help unload, so I might
as well catch a few more winks.

The sound of a salad plate being placed on the floor
woke me. Everything was back where it was supposed
to be, except my new diamond E. My hoomin had set
it next to my plate.

"I wasn't sure where you wanted me to put it," he
said as I picked it up.

"I haven't really thought about it," I confessed. I
looked over to where great grandpa's ring hung from a
nail on the wall above my bed. "Could you put it on a
shorter chain, so it hangs above the ring?"

My hoomin thought for a second. "Yeah, sure. I'd
have to stop somewhere and get one. There's a shop
down the block from the office, I will look there during
lunch tomorrow."

"Thank you. I'll leave it on my desk until then." I
carried the charm into my office and set it on my desk.
I briefly considered whether it would be wiser to stash
it in a drawer. Before this weekend, I never would
have considered an animal to be capable of stealing
something like that. My faith in the general goodness
of critters was definitely shaken.

I shook my head and left the charm on the desktop.
I finished my salad and hopped up to join my hoomin

on the couch. He had taken his dinner dishes back to the kitchen, and his lap was available for snuggling. As he stroked my fur from nose to poof, I fell asleep.